STAN
09/11

1 5 OCT 2011

1 2 NOV 2011

ABONO 12/14

THOR 9/18

EUE 10/19

PETERBOROUGH LIBRARIES

24 Hour renewal line 08458 505606

This book is to be returned on or before the latest date shown above, but may be renewed up to three times if the book is not in demand. Ask at your local library for details.

Please note that charges are ~ books

Also by Maryrose Wood
with the Duchess of Northumberland
THE POISON DIARIES

THE POISON DIARIES

NIGHTSHADE

BOOK II OF THE POISON DIARIES TRILOGY

by Maryrose Wood

BASED ON A CONCEPT BY

The Duchess of Northumberland

HarperCollins *Children's Books*

First published in paperback in Great Britain
by HarperCollins *Children's Books* 2011
HarperCollins *Children's Books* is a division
of HarperCollins*Publishers* Ltd
77-85 Fulham Palace Road, Hammersmith, London W6 8JB

Visit us on the web at www.harpercollins.co.uk

www.poisondiaries.com

Poison Diaries is a registered trademark of Poison Diaries Ltd.

Text copyright © Poison Diaries Ltd 2011

ISBN 978-0-00-736624-8

Poison Diaries Ltd reserves the right to be identified
as the author of this work.

Printed and bound in England by Clays Ltd, St Ives plc

For Ruta Rimas, with deepest thanks

"Weed… fills my head with tales from the ancient forests, tales so old that the trees themselves call them legends. It is as if a veil has been lifted from my eyes, and the world I have lived in all my sixteen years is revealed to be something else entirely, something so marvellous I could never have imagined it…"

– JESSAMINE LUXTON, *The Poison Diaries*

 **1**

I WAKE, AS I usually do, to the sound of Weed's voice. It rustles in my ear as I sleep. It skitters through my dreams like autumn leaves along the ground. My skin warms, my breath quickens. The memories come unbidden.

It is early spring, before I became ill. Weed and I are on one of our long rambles through the rolling green fields of Northumberland. He tells me strange fables, one after another, of a world where plants can speak, and all forms of life are of equal worth: humans, animals, and plants, too.

I laugh, because the tales are so marvellous. He turns to me, solemn-faced, and I explain my reaction.

"Marvellous? You may find them so. The trees are quite serious when they tell them."

"But it is only a tale, a story – even to the trees, is it not? Look, here is a lovely place for our picnic. Shall we stop?"

How foolish I was then. How wrong I was, about so many things.

I thought love was a rare orchid that bloomed only once – but once it bloomed, it bloomed forever.

I thought that with the death of my mother, so many years ago, the worst of my life had already come and gone.

I thought my father would protect me from harm.

Was I wrong about Weed as well? Every time I draw breath I catch the earth scent of him. I lie motionless in my bed, alone in my tower bedchamber. A summer breeze floats through the open shutters, and I feel the tenderness of his kiss.

The last time I saw him I was dying. My mind

2

flew with dark wings, and I looked down on my own pain-wracked body as if it belonged to another. I had nightmare visions of a strange prince who fed me poison, who wooed and tormented me, who showed me bloody scenes and unspeakable evils – evils wrought by my father.

My heart still pounds when I recall those hellish dreams. I thought I would not survive them. There were times I did not wish to.

More memories play on my half-closed eyelids as the morning sun tries to pry them open: Weed sitting at my bedside, spooning medicine to my lips. Wiping my brow. Gazing at me in love and grief, his moss-green eyes bright with tears.

Then he was gone. He lost hope and left. Too faithless to stay by my side until the end, he abandoned me at the worst point of my illness. That is what Father said, after my fever finally broke and I gasped and cried my way back to life, like a second birth.

"He is gone, and good riddance. He is a coward and a trickster. You are not the first maiden to be

3

fooled by such a scoundrel. Bear your shame alone now; marry your work, and forget him, for you will not see him again." Father said it coldly, and not without satisfaction.

Of course, what Father says cannot always be believed. But Weed is gone; that much is true. There has been no word, and now the summer draws to a close.

I stretch and turn beneath the cool linen sheet. I flex each limb and yawn, like a waking cat. Am I well? It is hard to say. In some ways I am stronger than I was. I am less trusting, less innocent. I have thoughts, sometimes, that I barely recognise as my own. I feel capable of things that I never would have dreamed of before.

I have even taken over my father's healing practice. I had to; Father is too busy now, or too indifferent, to tend to people's ills as he used to. With my knowledge of plants, it was not difficult to learn the basic cures, and they are most of what any healer needs. One fever, croup, or childbirth pang is much like another.

4

Once I walked through Northumberland hooded and silent, too shy to speak, too unimportant to approach. Now I am known and respected, and even a little bit feared. I do not mind that.

But there is an ache within, an empty place. My heart, once lush with joy, now lies fallow. Everything tastes like dust.

Weed, I have whispered a thousand times as I wandered alone through the meadows of Hulne Park. *Where are you? Why did you leave? When will you come back to me?* But the dull, ocean roar of the grass is the only answer I receive.

Tell him I love him still, I weep into the bark of an ancient pine. *Tell him for me, please.*

Still, I get no reply.

I long to drift back to sleep and bury myself in the bittersweet dream of all that I have lost. But I must rise and dress. It is Sunday.

Yes, I go to church on Sundays, now. I go alone, for my father worships no god but knowledge. The tested, proven theories of long-dead men, as recorded in the musty books in the Duke's library – those are his only sacred texts.

I myself have sometimes wondered what force could have put so many kinds of life on the earth, and made us need each other so, and hurt each other so, but I have not yet conceived of an answer. Still, to church I go, three miles on foot in the hot August haze. It is for my own protection. A woman who knows how to heal will always be suspected of witchcraft in these parts. The witch laws were struck down before I was born, but the people fear what they fear.

This is the north of England, after all; it is beautiful and raw here, and the land, the wind, and the sea have minds of their own. The people do, too. The north is not London, where the latest fashion is always best. In the north, the new is suspect, and the old ways die hard.

Like an apparition I glide silently into the chapel, so that everyone may see I am a virtuous and God-fearing young woman, and that my powers, such as they are, are drawn from nothing more sinister than a sprig of feverfew, a tisane of camomile, or a paste of crushed garlic and cloves.

"Good morning, Miss Luxton," the people murmur as I pass. "Good day and good health to you." When they ask about my father, and wonder why he no longer goes out, I say he is busy with his apothecary garden, or studying ancient cures at the Duke's library at Alnwick Castle. The truth is that since my recovery, his frequent dark moods have knitted themselves into a ceaseless gloom. He works day and night, in his study or in the garden. At mealtimes he is silent; when we pass each other in the hall, he barely looks at me.

I thought I was alone before, before Weed came and I had only Father's stern presence for company. Now Father is as lost to me as Weed is.

I sit stiff-backed in a pew, not far from the church doors. I stand when the preacher asks us to stand. I kneel when he tells us to kneel. When it is time to sing hymns, I raise my voice with the congregation, not so loudly that I draw attention to myself, but with enough force to be heard.

When the service is over I linger, my head bowed. Those who would beg my help approach me in turn: "Miss Luxton, the baby won't stop coughing." "Miss Luxton, a week's come and gone and the wound won't heal." "Miss Luxton, it's near my time, I need something to ease the birth pangs, will you come right away if I send my girl for you?"

One after another they tell me their aches, their pains, their worries. I nod in sympathy and promise to come when needed. Then I follow my fellow worshippers through the door, stepping from the cool, damp air of the church into the merciless noonday sun.

The preacher speaks to each one of us as we exit, gazing into our eyes, clasping our hands. He tells us to believe, so that we may be saved. "Hellfire is a *thousand* times hotter than this," he warns, shaking a finger to the sky. "A *thousand* times a thousand! But you must believe!"

Outside the church the people gather in small,

frightened groups and whisper, "The end of the world is nigh."

They are righter than they know.

There – it has happened again. The words appear in my mind as if someone spoke them aloud. But there is no one here. It is as if my thoughts are not entirely my own.

And the voice – it chills my blood to admit it – but I have come realise that I know that voice. It is the voice from my nightmares. The voice of the evil prince.

He calls himself Oleander. The Prince of Poisons.

Shaken, I walk home from church, lay down my light summer shawl, eat a simple lunch of bread and cheese, alone. The cottage is quiet. Father must be out wandering the fields, or brooding behind the tall gate of his locked garden.

Once I thought of it as his apothecary garden, but now I know better. Those plants are poison, and the garden is something unnatural – a living weapon. Weed told me as much.

Your father has done me a great service, planting that garden. I hope he is not fool enough to think he is its master.

The words snake through my head, slow and inexorable, like oil spreading over water.

If so, he will pay the price someday, for that garden already has a master. One who will allow no pretenders to the throne.

There is a rap at the door.

I startle. Am I losing my mind? Is the dark prince of my nightmares standing outside my cottage this instant?

A charming thought, lovely. But I have no need of doors. All the locked gates in the world could not contain me. I enter when and where I wish. I hold the key to every poisoned heart.

The rap comes again, insistent. I remember the woman at church, the one who was heavy with child. Perhaps her pains have started. Trying to shake off this strange bout of madness, I grab my shawl and my medical bag and hurry to the door.

"I am ready," I begin to say, but two men stand

before me. Local men, both farmers. I have seen them before, at market day. Their awkward bulk fills the doorframe and blocks the slanted afternoon light.

"Miss Luxton?"

"Yes."

The taller man glances at the bag in my hands. "Might we come in for a moment and speak with you? It won't take long."

I bid them enter and show them to the parlour, but I remain standing. "I would ask you to sit, but as you see I was just on my way out," I say, gesturing with my bag. "I trust you are not ill? That is the usual reason for strangers to appear at my door."

The men shake their heads and glance uncomfortably around the room, with its vaulted ceiling and tall, arched windows. Long ago this cottage was a chapel. Now it is our home. *Is that why I am being curse with this strange madness?* I think. *Can the echo of a thousand unanswered prayers ever truly fade? Can a chapel be haunted?*

My uneasy visitors wring their hats in their hands.

11

The tall man speaks. "Sorry to detain you, Miss Luxton. We're from the Association for the Prosecution of Criminal Acts and Undesirables. Me and Horace, here, we're making enquiries in the neighbourhood, regarding the matter of – well, a missing person, you might say."

"Dead person, he means." His companion scowls. "Don't drag this out, Ned, I'll be wanting supper soon, and it's a long way home on foot."

Missing person – dead person. Surely they cannot mean Weed? I bite my lip hard, and use the pain to steady myself.

The one called Ned swallows and nods. "Miss Luxton, there was a travelling preacher who came and went through these parts. 'Repent, repent,' you know the type – anyways, the man hasn't been seen for some time. A week ago his Bible turns up near the crossroads, buried deep in a hedge of bramble. A farmer from Alnwick found it. One of his lambs got tangled up in the thorns, see, and he had to cut out the branches to free it. It was a bit worse for the rain

12

and sun – the Bible, I mean – but you could still read the name on the flyleaf."

Ned pauses and wipes his face with a simple cotton square he extracts from a pocket. "Forgive me, miss. There's more, but it's not an easy story to tell to a young lady like yourself. Not far from the Bible was… was…"

"A pile of bones," Horace interrupts. "Human bones. Picked so clean you'd think they'd been boiled for soup." He cleans his teeth with his own dirty fingernail, as if to demonstrate.

His words bore into me, releasing a gush of dread from some deep reservoir inside. "The ravens of Hulne Park do their work swiftly," I say, masking my fear. "I hope you will follow their good example, gentlemen. Why are you here?"

"The truth is, miss, we don't much care what happened to this fellow. Good riddance, one might say. Who wants to hear all that gloom and doom? But as it turns out, the preacher had a wife, and they both were members of our association. Dues paid in full." Horace shakes his head in disappointment. "Which means that we two are stuck with the job of investigating."

"Couldn't happen at a worse time, either," Ned adds. "Right in the middle of the harvest."

"Was it murder?" I say the word as if it meant nothing horrible – *murder, murder, murder* – a word like any other.

Horace snorts, a contemptuous laugh. "A man's bleached bones don't just fall out of the sky, do they?"

"God alone knows what happened." Ned rolls his eyes heavenward. "And God alone metes final justice. But that don't mean we can shut our eyes to this business. The association must perform its duty, Miss Luxton. That's why we're here. Allow me to ask: Do you have any knowledge of this matter? Firsthand, secondhand, or otherwise?"

"I do not."

"Duly noted. Like we said, we've been making enquiries. We were told there was a young man living here. May we speak to him?"

I hesitate. "Why?"

14

They glance at each other before Horace replies. "The widow's paid her dues. That means we have to find someone to prosecute. Otherwise the case'll drag on and on, and we'll never have a moment's peace. We could pay her to drop it, but that'd cost us a king's ransom."

The two men stand there, fingering their hats, waiting for my answer. Deliberately I remove my shawl and take a seat. I must, for my legs have begun to tremble.

"So you wish to find some poor fool to charge with a crime? Whether or not he is guilty of it?" My voice is cool, my anger palpable – how like my father I sound!

"Guilty, innocent – it don't have to be so formal as all that!" Horace smiles. "No doubt it was an accident, whatever happened. Words get exchanged. Push comes to shove. The preacher ends up with a bloody nose in the dirt. Your friend goes on his merry way, as any of us would, and that's the last he thinks of it. How was he to know the preacher could die of such a feeble blow?"

To demonstrate, Ned cuffs Horace on the head. For a moment I wonder if I am about to witness a murder myself, but Horace grits his teeth and continues.

"We take your friend to the magistrate, where he apologises most sincerely and pleads the benefit of clergy. Then he stands there like a good lad while he gets his pardon."

"A pardon?" I interject. "But a man is dead. Surely his widow will want justice. I would, if I were her."

"Every man worth his salt loses his temper now and again. That's how the magistrate'll see it, you can be sure. It gets the widow off our backs and puts the whole matter to bed. We'll pay your friend a day's wages for his trouble, too."

Ned grins; his teeth are yellow as a mule's. "But there won't be no hanging, that we can promise you."

"Lay off the talk of hanging, you dumb ox, you're going to frighten the girl." Horace turns back to me. "Now that we've laid your worries to rest – can we speak to the young fellow?"

I stand and move to the window. "The youth you

16

refer to goes by the name of Weed. He stayed here with us for a short while. He was a great help to my father with the work in the gardens. But he no longer lives here, and I have no knowledge of his whereabouts."

I let my eyes drift downward, shy and maidenly. "I would like to speak to him as well. He left soon after" – I allow my voice to catch with emotion; why not? – "soon after my father suggested that we become engaged."

My visitors exchange a look. They too were young men, once. And now that they know how I have been shamed and abandoned, perhaps they will leave me be.

"I see." Horace's voice is gruff. "Perhaps it would be best if we spoke to your father, then."

"My father is out." I wave my hand, as if to indicate the whole north of England and Scotland, too. "If you can find him, by all means, speak to him. Feel free to go outside and look. I will make tea while you do."

Before they can catch breath enough to answer, I excuse myself and leave. How convenient it is to be a woman, sometimes! One can always use the kitchen as an excuse to escape men's tedious conversations, their scheming and planning. *Father has his work to hide behind*, I think, *and I have my kettle.*

As I light the fire my mind wanders down strange paths. Dread churns within me – dread that, somehow, this preacher's death has something to do with Weed's disappearance. But what?

I take my metal canister of tea off the shelf. It is my own mixture of dried lavender blossoms and lemon balm, harvested from my garden and hung in the storeroom to dry. *Weed helped me hang these stalks*, I think. *His hands touched these tender leaves, just as they touched me…*

I measure the tea, crumbling the dried leaves through my fingers to release the sweet fragrance. As I do, I think how easy it would be to add a bit of this and that to the kettle – just enough to sicken my guests later on, when they are safe at home in their beds, with only their wives nearby to hear their cries. Or enough to kill them, and silence their annoying questions forever.

I do nothing of the kind, of course. Even after all

I have seen, all I have suffered, all I have lost, I still know the difference between right and wrong.

Do you really, lovely? I find the distinction rather blurry, myself.

I am a healer, I think, blocking out the voice of evil. *I will not kill.*

But it is oddly comforting to know that I can.

2

20th August

This morning I treated a bad case of sunburn,
rheumy eyes, and a deep wound made by a rusted
nail that a careless farmer stepped upon. The
last was the most serious, but if the farmer soaks
his foot in a strong brew of sage and yarrow as I
instructed, it ought to heal quickly.

In the afternoon I tended my kitchen garden,
which shows signs of fatigue from this relentless
heat. As do I, it seems. I wait in dread for the

voice of Oleander to return. So far it has not.

I hope I am not going mad.

ALL DAY AND LATE into the evening, the fields ring with the sound of reaping. The scythe swings, and like solders grievously overmatched in battle, the grass falls, row after slaughtered row.

I witnessed it myself this morning, as I walked from farm to farm, dispensing cures, advice, and comfort. Now, as I sit here sewing, I try to imagine what Weed might have heard, if he had walked beside me – the cries of protest, perhaps, as the scythe swings once more.

Does the wheat despise us? I find myself wondering. *Does it wish we were the ones slain?*

My thoughts are scattered by a sharp sound, the pop and hiss of wood catching fire in the parlour hearth. That log, too, was once the living limb of a tree – perhaps one of the ancient ones from the forest, with their noble, spreading branches and strange tales.

"A fire in summer," I say without looking up from

my sewing. "Surely that is a waste of wood."

Father straightens from the hearth with a grunt. "There is a storm on the way. When the wind howls like this, warmth is required." He takes his chair and gazes into the flames. "I am worried about your health, Jessamine. Until now I have said nothing, trusting that time would be the best remedy, but my concern bids me speak at last."

"Speak, then." Already I am on my guard.

"It has been some time since your illness passed. To outward appearances you seem recovered, and go about your work without complaint." Thoughtful, he gazes into the fire. "But there are days you lie late in your bed, as if reluctant to wake. Your skin is pale, but now and then your cheeks flush red, perhaps recalling some secret shame. At times you stare blindly into the air, as if conversing with phantoms. The stain of tears is ever present on your face."

"There is no need to worry." Anger kindles within me, but I will be cautious: My father must have some reason of his own for speaking this way. "My body is perfectly well."

"Your body is young and strong, and can survive much. But what of your heart, Jessamine?"

I put down my needle and thread. "My heart will heal when Weed comes back."

"I think not. I think your heart will only begin to mend when you accept that Weed is gone." Finally he looks up from the fire and faces me. "Gone, and never to return."

"I don't believe you." If he wishes to provoke me, he is succeeding. "Time and again you have told me that Weed left me – heartlessly ran off as I lay dying. Before I did not have the strength to argue. Now I do."

"Calm yourself – "

"Weed loves me. If he is keeping away from me, there must be a reason."

"I have told you the reason. He is a common scoundrel, who despoiled and abandoned you in the most unforgivable manner – "

"You have told me lies. For I know Weed would be at my side even now, unless some force was preventing him."

"You have not had any word from him at all, then?"

"No. I have not."

Father looks at me, strangely satisfied, and I realise, *This is what he wanted – to know if I have heard from Weed. Why would he wish to know that?*

I feel exposed, and look away to hide the tears that spring to my eyes.

Such passion! Such grief! It is most enticing, my lovely. A pity you waste it on that ridiculous boy, that callow, unwanted Weed...

The room sways. I clutch my head.

"What is it, Jessamine? You look unwell. Let me prepare a tonic for you."

I am faint, but I will not admit that to Father. He pours something for me to drink and brings it to me. The glass hovers in front of me. In its swirl of liquid I see visions: *A dying lamb. The madhouses of London. A pair of large, terrifying wings.*

I push the glass away. "I had terrible dreams when I was ill, Father," I say in a low voice. "Some of them

24

were about you. About what you did on your trips to London."

His eyes glitter in the firelight. "Take a sip, my dear. It will steady you."

"I dreamed that you went to the madhouse there. That you fed poison to the lunatics, in order to test your formulas."

He stands so quickly the drink spills. "How strange. The fantasies our minds concoct when we are sick...."

I rise to my feet, clawing at my head as if I could tear that voice out by its roots. "A fantasy? I thought so, too. Now I am not so sure."

Careful, lovely... your father has a dreadful temper, you know....

I watch the blue vein on his forehead throb. His words are calm, but his voice is a tightened sinew of rage. "Jessamine, it seems your mind is more affected by your illness than I first supposed. I suggest you go to bed. I know some cures that can help you."

"Your cures!" I practically spit with contempt. "I

25

think your cures are poison, Father. I think everything you have told me is a lie, and that which I believed to be a dream is all too real."

The images take form again – me, flying high over the fields of Northumberland, born aloft by a pair of dark wings. "And Weed's love for me, and mine for him, is the realest thing of all," I gasp. "If you will not tell me where he is, then I will have to look for him myself."

"Enough." Three strides, and he is across the room. "I will tell you what you wish to know. But I warn you, you may regret it." He gestures for me to sit down. "During your illness, Weed became distraught. Because of his extraordinary talent for healing, I believe he felt responsible for curing you, and was driven mad with frustration when he could not. He grew agitated, unreasonable. Finally he left. I could not chase after him, for I did not dare leave your side. You were at death's very threshold that night."

The light of the fire glows behind my father, casting lurid shadows along the stone floor. "He abandoned you, Jessamine, and you should despise him for it, not pine for his return. But you are right to call me a liar: He did not simply run off, as I have told you in the past."

I sit there, unmoving as a statue in church, as Father's voice drops deep. "You were so weak. I thought it would kill you to know the truth. As time passed and you regained your strength, I dared hope you would make your peace with my story and would never have to know the fate of that coward Weed. I prayed you would forget about him. He fooled us both, for a time. I do not blame you for being deceived by him. I was deceived as well."

The flames leap, and the shadows do their mocking dance. My father's words toll like a bell.

"Weed is dead. He hanged himself, in a remote part of the woods of Hulne Park. I found the body myself. The fool!"

Father approaches me and places a hand on my shoulder. I allow myself to soften, to weep. It is not difficult. I shed tears at will these days.

"I thought it would be too cruel to tell you the truth. But it is crueller still to let you go on longing for something that can never be." He steps back and spreads his arms, as if waiting for me to step into his embrace. "I hope you can forgive me, Jessamine. Oh, the curse of being a parent! The sins we commit to ease our children's suffering!"

I rise from the chair. Father takes a step toward me. I wheel from his open arms and race outside, into the storm.

"Jessamine – " His voice follows me to the door, but the moment I am outside the shrieking wind drowns out every sound but the pounding of my own heart. Let Father run after me if he dares. I am one with the storm now, wild and furious, a howl of rage.

"Weed!" I hurl my desperate cry to the starless sky. Up the twisting path I climb. The ground is muck beneath my feet. Am I truly mad, then? I must be, to think the poison garden is the only place left for me to turn.

But how else will I finally discover what is real?

How else will I know what is true, and what is a lie?

And when the worst has already happened, what is left to fear?

Unless the worst is yet to come. The thought stops me short. I pause for breath. Eyes closed, I feel the earth spin drunkenly beneath my feet, slipped off its axis like a wheel on a broken axle.

Foolish Jessamine… did you really think I was only a dream?

Thunder cracks, loud as a gunshot. I press my hand to my chest. My heart flutters like a trapped bird within the cage of my bones. My hair hangs sodden, like seaweed trailing from the ropes of a sailing ship. My dress is as wet as if I had risen up from the German Ocean and walked ashore.

"Help me," I cry with all the ragged breath I have left. "If you are here, show yourself, I beg you. For I do not know what to believe anymore."

I will show you.

Once more, lightning slashes crookedly across the sky, briefly revealing the path before the world plunges

29

into darkness again. The wind howls and blows, not east to west, but in strange circles that seem as if they would pluck the trees straight up from the ground and hurl them down again like broken toys.

The black gate of the poison garden looms before me. I hurl myself at the unyielding bars. The lock taunts me, an iron apple dangling from a lifeless tree. Exhausted, I collapse to the ground.

I assure you, I am no dream, lovely. I have powers you cannot imagine. I can help you find what you seek. All you need do is ask.

Help me, my heart begs, yet I dare not speak the name of the one to whom I plead. The horrors of my nightmares come back to me ten times over: the torment. The lunatic asylum. My father's wickedness and murderous lies.

Nothing about this world is what I thought it was. I am lost, and have only one refuge.

"Oleander!" I cry, but the wind swallows all sound. I lift myself from the mud and seize the bars of the gate in my two hands. The wet metal is cold and rough against my cheek. "Please! I need you. I need you to show me the truth… as you did once before…"

The sound of the storm changes. To each side of me rain pours, lightning cracks, wind howls. Somehow I am shielded.

I throw my head back and search the sky. Directly above me the night takes form. It is darkness upon darkness, like ink spilled upon black velvet.

The inky stain is in the shape of outspread wings.

I have waited for you to come back to me, the Prince of Poisons croons. *And now you are here.*

"Tell me, please," I gasp. The shadow wings beat once, twice. "Is Weed dead or alive?"

Your beloved Crabgrass is rather unkempt at the moment. In a foul temper, and in urgent need of a bath. But yes; he is alive.

The relief I feel is mixed with the sure, sickening knowledge that my father is no more than a murderous villain.

"I must find him – does my father know where he is?"

If your father knew where to find Weed, he would have had him killed by now. He cannot harness Weed's

31

gifts for his own purposes, and he will not have him be a potential rival.

"He is a monster! Oleander, can you help me find Weed?"

I can if I choose to. But first you must prove yourself worthy.

"Tell me what to do."

I want you to avenge your mother's death. Bring justice to her killer. Then you will have earned my aid.

My heart clenches. "My mother was murdered? By whom?"

Who do you think, lovely?

His laughter falls like a rain of ice. *There is no end to the wickedness of humans, is there? It surprises even me, sometimes. When your task is done, then I will help you find what you seek. And you will help me in exchange, when the time comes. For you and I need each other, as you will someday learn...*

"What do you mean?" I cry, but the shadow being ascends to the vault of the night, and is gone.

The rain pours down with doubled fury. I slip and

stumble along the muddy path, back to the cottage, too shocked to even weep.

My whole life has been based on lies. And the only being that can help me find Weed is an incarnation of evil itself.

Have I made a terrible mistake in rousing the dark prince? It does not matter, for I must find Weed again, whatever the price.

And, this, too I swear: No corrupt magistrate, no dim-witted committee of farmers, will stand in judgment of my mother's killer.

No. I will deal with him – with Father – myself.

The door to the cottage opens with a push. The fire sputters as the water from my clothes streams across the stone floor and sizzles into the hearth.

"Father?" He is not here. Is he out searching for me in the storm? Has he been crushed by a tree or trapped on the far side of a flooding stream?

I hope not. For I would hate to miss the chance to take my own vengeance.

And yet, there is some small doubt within me. My father is wicked, I know. A liar and a murderer. But I always believed he loved my mother. There was a warmth in his voice, a softness in his eyes, that only ever appeared when he spoke of her.

Surely it would not be wrong to want proof, I think.

I walk toward the study, wet feet slapping against stone. The door is unlocked and swings open as I approach. Every window shutter has blown open. Gusts of wind howl through the room, lifting papers, toppling books. I can scarcely see, but who could light a candle in this maelstrom?

As if in answer, lightning flashes once more, and then again. A volume lies open on Father's desk. Its pages tremble in the moving air, begging me to read them.

I lay a hand on the open page. As I do, the wind ceases and the night goes silent and still. In this otherworldly calm I can finally light a candle to read by. The page is written in my father's hand, although his familiar neat script is slanted pell-mell and blotted, as if he wrote in a terrible rush, or as if his thoughts had become tinged with madness…

> …*my life's work is lost, utterly lost, or so it seems. I think of all that I sacrificed to gain this knowledge, so painstakingly recorded in my diary. What compelled that misbegotten freak to seize the record of my work and flee? As if he had any need for it! Someday I will pay him back, I swear it – I will find him, wherever he hides, and reclaim what is mine.*
>
> *So much suffering, for naught! So many lives sacrificed! Even yours, my darling, my Elizabeth… but how was I to know that the child in your womb would weaken you so severely? You were never the same after the birth; it was as if all your strength was used to nourish the child, at your own expense. Poor Jessamine. She scarcely remembers you. She would never suspect how I think of you hourly, write you these letters every night, and above all, continue our work…*

She has grown so like you it startles me. Would
you be proud to know how well she endured
my treatments, Elizabeth? She suffered, yes, but
survived greater doses than I ever dared give you.

It occurs to me now: Perhaps her physiology
has some special tolerance for the dark substances,
since she was first exposed while still in your
womb… this may be a topic for further study.

Here is all the proof I need.

My father poisoned my mother. She let him do it,
it seems. She was a willing part of his "work," even as
I grew within her belly. Still, he bears full blame for
her death.

And my illness was no strong fever, my recovery no
miracle cure wrought by the skills of Thomas Luxton.
My father poisoned me, and harbours not one speck of
remorse for doing so.

And Weed – Weed is alive. Somewhere. And my
father will kill him someday, if he can. If I do not stop
him first, that is.

Truth, terrible truth! It is like an ancient curse, from which there is no escape. The truth will drive one mad. Yet without it, how can one make sense of life's madness?

Do you like the task I set you, lovely?

I do. For now I know who I am.

I am Jessamine Luxton. Poison ran in my veins before I was born.

I know how to cure. And I know how to kill.

I have tried for so long to be good, but there is no need to fight my destiny anymore.

I am my father's daughter, after all.

A STAND OF HEMLOCK water dropwort grows in a sturdy group near the edge of a stream, deep in the old forest of Northumberland. The plants have straight, thick, hollow stems, topped with lacy flowers. One of their fleshy roots would kill me, if I were fool enough to eat it.

"Such delicious roots," the plant hums. "Sweet and rich and filling, Master Weed. Are you sure you do not want a taste?"

"Have you any shame?" I roll to my side on this soggy bed of moss. "Look at you. Your leaves masquerade as parsley. Your stalks as celery. Your roots as parsnip. How many men have you killed with your trickery?"

"Not just men. Women. Children. Cattle, too." The lace-caps of blooms flutter, all innocence. "You seem angry, fleshbody. Perhaps living in the forest does not suit you after all."

I shift my position, trying to find a dry spot. After a night of wild storms, everything is wet: the ground, the trees, the rocks. Mushrooms sprout in every crevice. Some of them, too, are killers, but they know better than to boast about it.

"It is not the forest that irks me. It is your pride in your own wickedness. You gain nothing from killing. You take no nourishment from your prey, as the hawks and foxes do. Yet you do it with enjoyment."

"We act as it is in our nature to act. Just as you do, Human Who Hears."

This is what they call me in the forest. The fleshbody. The Human Who Hears. Even here I am made to feel like a freak.

"After all, you too, have killed," the dropwort adds.

39

"And there was no nourishment involved. Was there?"

I do not answer. For yes, I have killed. Shamefully I have taken innocent life. And I would kill again, right now, if I had the means.

My victims would be two in number: Thomas Luxton, father of my beloved Jessamine. And Oleander, the Prince of Poisons.

It is for Jessamine's sake alone that I stay away.

Of its own will, my hand strays to the book of evil I carry with me day and night. Thomas Luxton's book of poisons. It is wrapped safe and dry in a square of oilcloth I stole from a farm wife's washing line.

Every day I swear I will burn it. It is like that wicked garden of his: something unnatural that should never have been created. But I cannot bring myself to do it. It is the one link I have to the past – to all that was stolen from me. To happiness. To Jessamine.

"Answer, fleshbody. Do not ignore, like an ordinary half-sensed human. We know you can hear us."

"Yes, I can." I rake pebbles into my hand with my

fingers and toss them one by one against a large out-cropping of rock. They bounce off the stone, narrowly missing my delicate, deadly accuser. "Alone among my kind, I can hear you. But that does not mean I am interested in what you have to say."

The notched leaves flare in outrage. I feel pleasure at their hurt. This is the sort of creature I have become. Bitter. Angry. With too little respect for others, and far too much pity for myself.

I rise to leave. It makes the plants angry that I can do that. Walk away.

"Listen to the fleshbody," the dropwort retorts. "A mere seventeen turns of the seasons on this ancient earth of ours, and yet he dismisses us. What is your answer, coward? Have you killed, or have you not killed?"

Through a canopy of alder leaves I glance up at the sky. It is grey, and thick with clouds. I half expect to see a shadow in the shape of wings, blotting out what little light is left. A gash of nothingness inked across the heavens.

"Yes. I have," I snarl. "We are killers both. Do not make me prove it."

With the poison diary under my arm, I turn and run.

"What do you hope to find in the forest, flesh-body? She is not here, you know!"

I plug my ears and run faster, deeper into the woods.

Jessamine once told me that humans go for walks in the forest to be alone and "collect their thoughts." At the time I did not understand what she meant. Why would human thoughts be scattered among the trees?

For me, being in the forest is like going to market day at Alnwick, but instead of people's elbows jostling me, it is the low branches whipping across my face, leaves sticking to my hair, roots rising up to trip me.

There is no place to hide from the trees. They know everything I do – every grouse I kill to eat, every sip I take from the stream, every shelter I build for myself of leaves and moss. I cannot move behind a laurel to make water but they are there.

Most often they speak according to their kind – the deep rumble of oak, the whisper of the birch, or the singsong chant of the alder. The evergreen stands of pine have voices sharp as needles.

But the forest can speak as one, when it must. When the trees so choose, they think with one mind. When there is danger, especially, they speak in one voice of a thousand echoes.

I hate it when they do this. For the forest mind is always right, and will hear no argument.

I climb uphill, following the path of a stream. Its trickle soothes me. When I am thirsty, I stop and kneel to drink.

You have spent half a season with us, Weed. And you are still unhappy. Filled with rage. We do not know how to help you.

"You cannot help me." I splash water on my face, again and again, but I cannot cool off. "My love has been taken from me. I have promised to stay away, and I can never be happy again."

Seasons change, Weed, the forest says. *Seasons change.*

I find my way to where the stream opens up to a quiet pool. Stripping myself of my stolen clothes, I gulp a breath and dive in. It feels good to use my muscles and to feel the cool water against my skin, but even that does little to soothe my temper.

I have the body of a man now, but of what use is my strength? I have already failed at being human. That I go on, hiding in this deep forest like an outcast, belonging nowhere, banished and alone, is a mystery even to me.

After I climb out I sit on the bank and stare at my reflection. It is the only human face I have looked at since fleeing to the forest. My hair is long and tangled, and my cheeks are covered with a rough growth of beard. My skin is brown from the sun and the dirt. In my eyes there is loneliness and a cold glint of fury.

I toss in a stone, and the image shatters. When I was a child, taunted for my oddness and scorned by other people, I often thought that if I could only live

44

among the plants, I would be happy. Now I am here, and all I feel is rage.

Do not deceive yourself, Weed. Your anger is not for us. It lives within you.

Enough. I shake the water drops from my wild hair like a dog, and head for the clearing at the highest point of the woods. At least there I can see the sky and get away from this chattering canopy of leaves. But the lecture follows me as I stumble and climb.

Your ears have the power to hear us, but your heart is bitter as a rhubarb leaf. This bitterness makes you deaf to the truth…

"Leave me be," I growl, kicking at a root.

You have erred, Weed. That is why you suffer. You chose one being and elevated her above the others, as if all life did not have the same worth. You did terrible things for her sake – for the sake of the human girl, the one with the golden hair, yellow as a flower –

Jessamine. The leaves flutter her name. The air shimmers with the sound. It pierces me like a thorn.

Remember, Weed: The good of one tree is not

45

important. The good of the forest is what matters.

"Enough!" I press my hands to my ears; will they ever let me be? "Humans do not think as you think. They – we – do not feel the way you feel."

We know.

"And not all plants are so selfless and noble as you describe. There is evil in the human world, and evil in the plant world, too."

Throughout the forest, the leaves go perfectly still. It is a silence that is most unnatural.

We know, says the mind of the forest. *All too well, we know.*

On bruised hands and raw knees I continue my climb, to the flattened ridge that rises past the edge of the wood. The clearing on the hilltop is small, compared to the rolling meadows of Hulne Park. It is an open field of high moorland, with clumps of rough grass surrounding a low growth of heath and a blanket bog of peat.

The grey clouds hang heavy and low. Still, it is a

relief to be at least a little distance from the trees, and to see the open sky.

The cloudberries are ripe. The crowberries are, too. I help myself to the amber and purple fruits. The plants do not mind that I harvest from them, for it is how they spread their seed. They hum with pride when I choose the plumpest berries from each and praise their sweetness.

I follow the stream as it cuts through the centre of the clearing. Soon I hear a familiar chant.

Touch me, touch me not. Touch me, touch me not.

If I were not in such a bad temper, the tune would make me smile. At the damp edge of the far side of the clearing, near where the stream disappears back into the forest, grow those whom I call, for lack of a better word, my friends. These simple flowers are my only pleasant companions. Their talk has the power to soothe my unhappiness, the same way the sap from their stems soothes the itch from a nettle scratch.

They grow in a tidy cluster, with upright stems. Even now, in late summer, when darkness falls earlier every night, the touch-me-nots are covered with blooms. The bell-shaped orange-yellow blossoms droop under the broad leaves, like ladies shading themselves beneath green parasols.

On calmer days, the reddish spots on their petals have made me think of the golden freckles that would bloom on Jessamine's skin after a walk in the sun. Right now they remind me of other things: scarlet pinpricks left by a hungry bite. A spatter of fresh blood on dry earth. The mottled flush of a killing fever, dappled across a pale, beloved cheek.

I step around the prickly heath and stretch out on the soft peat. I watch the speckled blossoms bob and dance, and feel my clenched fists loosen.

"The forest is angry with me," I say. "Everywhere I go, I am scolded."

The touch-me-nots murmur sympathy, then fall silent. They were made to offer balm. It is why I seek them out.

"Tell me," I say after a while. "Tell me what is happening at Hulne Abbey." Not often, but sometimes, the touch-me-nots have news for me. From Jessamine's kitchen garden at the cottage, the potted lilies on the altar at her church, the sheep meadows that cover the slopes of Hulne Park where she walks, the morning glories that twine around the shutters of her bedchamber window – now and then they send word, whispered from one plant to another, until it arrives at my ear.

Each time the news has been the same. *She is well. There is a changed hue to her eyes – they were once a soft, trusting blue, but now they are the colour of ice. There is something unyielding in the carriage of her spine. But she is alive, and strong.*

If she were not, Thomas Luxton would be a dead man. But as long as she thrives, I will accept my fate. I will obey Oleander's command and stay away. I will live like an animal, or a beggar. I will spend my life among the plants, or alone. It does not matter. As long as she is safe.

"Any news at all?" I ask again. With less murder in my voice, this time.

The touch-me-nots do not answer.

"How is Jessamine?" I demand to know. "Where is she?"

"If you wish to know, why not go and see for yourself?" They say it without ire. I shake my head.

"I cannot go back among the humans again."

"Because of the girl?"

"I am ruined by what I did for her sake. I killed a man, a foolish man who wished me no harm, and the change of seasons will not bring him back. The humans will never forgive me for that."

"Death is final among them." They say it as if understanding, but they cannot understand, really.

"It has not been easy for you, living in the forest," they add, after a while.

"No."

"It is not easy for the forest, either."

"I ask nothing of the forest, except to be left alone."

The light is fading. A scatter of leaves blows across the moor, red and yellow and brown.

"It is time for you to go back, Weed."

I do not wish to hear this.

"The forest marches slowly, in step with the

seasons. All is rhythm, patience, stillness…"

Their true meaning remains unspoken. But I hear it, plain as the chilling wind that even now rushes across this hilltop moor: It is better to be like the plants than like me. For I am rootless. Angry. Abrupt. Alone.

"You are a disturbance to the world of the forest," they say, in that gentle, tinkling voice. "You are unsettled, and filled with passions we do not understand. You must return to your own kind. Go back to the humans. Settle your affairs with them, in whatever way they do. Pay the price for your deeds."

"I came to you for comfort. Instead – more banishment." I stand, but where can I run to this time? From this high outlook I can see across the forest canopy to the turrets of Alnwick Castle in the distance, perched on the embankment, overlooking the twisting river Aln. The stone battlements blend into the grey sky. Torches burn in the watchtowers, glowing like red-hot coals.

"I cannot go back," I say, my voice cracking. "Oleander made me swear I would not go back. On

51

Jessamine's life, I swore."

"Oleander!" The touch-me-nots tremble in rage. "The human apothecary has done this! He brought the wicked plants together. He gave them a home where they should not have a home. He let them twine together in a way nature would never have permitted. Oleander was one of us, once. Now he is a great danger to you. To you. To all of us."

A gust of wind whirls across the flattened hill, making all the plants quake. After it passes, the touch-me-nots continue to shiver – now, it seems, in fear. "You must go back. Go back to the place you call Hulne Abbey. To that doomed place, where the dreadful garden grows."

"Is it Jessamine? Has she been harmed?"

The flowers sound panicked. "Go. Go see for yourself."

4

30th August

I have made an early start today. I have already
packed a satchel with lunch and water, for I am off
to go collecting, in the distant fields and along the
woodland edges. I expect I will find everything I
need there.

It seems odd that I must walk for miles in
search of the specimens I need, when so many of
their kind grow in abundance close by. But to take
what I need from Father's garden is too dangerous;

he keeps the key on his belt, and the theft would
never go unnoticed. I will not risk detection now.
I am not afraid. I am, to be honest, excited.
Tonight at supper, I will do what I have sworn to do.
Then my mother's death will be avenged. And
– if Oleander keeps his word – my own life can
truly begin.

IT IS LATE AFTERNOON when I return, though the sky is so grey with clouds it seems more like dusk. I bathe the filth of the day from me, for I am as covered in earth as a grave-digger, and change into a fresh gown. Everything I do is ordinary, yet extraordinary at the same time. Never have I gone about these everyday tasks knowing what I now know, or planning what I now plan.

Once dressed, I prepare to do the most ordinary task of all, one I have done all my life: make dinner for my father.

I take my time, for it is a special pleasure to cook during the harvest season, when every ingredient is at its peak. I prepare small game hens, poached in a seasoned consommé of my own devising. Herbed new potatoes, creamed spinach, and a clove-scented pudding. I set the table as if for an honoured guest.

When everything is ready, I cover the food and retreat to my kitchen garden to pray. I know there is no god who would condone what I am about to do. But the spirits of the dead might feel otherwise.

"Was it for love of him that you did it, Mother?" I murmur into my folded hands. "Did it blind you to the truth, and make you willing to endanger yourself, and your unborn child, just to please him?"

The breeze blows but bears no answer. None is needed. I already know how passion can drive one to do the unthinkable. I myself am proof enough of that.

"Forgive me," I whisper. "I know vengeance cannot bring back the dead. If you loved him, you must despise me for what I now do. But the living need justice, too."

I brush the dirt from my knees and return inside. There is a man in the parlour.

"Miss Luxton, is it? I remember you. My, you've grown up a bit over the summer, haven't you?"

He turns, and my heart freezes. I could never forget that face. It is Tobias Pratt, proprietor of a nearby asylum. The horrible man who first delivered Weed to our door, as if he were nothing more than a bundle of rags.

"My father is not at home," I say quickly. "I cannot receive you, Mr. Pratt. Come back another day."

"Not so fast, miss. I'm here for my payment. If my sources tell me right, your father owes me a bit of money." He laughs. "A fair bit, I'd say."

Could this idiot have come at a worse possible time? "Money?" I say, feigning casualness. "As payment for what?"

"For that green-eyed wretch Weed, of course! Didn't the brat turn out to be useful? Him and his strange witch-boy ways, always talking to himself and creating strange concoctions. When I left him here I told your father I'd be back, and then he could decide what the lad was worth to him and pay up accordingly." Pratt pulls a chair from the table and sits down. "That's how honourable men do business, see? No need for a contract, a simple handshake will do."

He belches and licks his fingers. "Pardon me. I confess, Miss Luxton, this dinner you had set out on the table smelled so good, I took a fork and plate from the kitchen and helped myself to a taste while I was waiting. It's a long, hungry ride from the asylum, and a man has to keep up his strength. Don't worry, there's still plenty left for you and your pa." He pats his belly contentedly. "I could surely go for a pint of ale, though."

I lift the lid of the chafing dish. One drumstick, three potatoes, and a generous spoonful of creamed spinach, gone.

"You're a fine cook, miss. You'll make a good wife some day for some lucky chap. In fact, I might point out that I'm a bachelor myself, and a prosperous business owner, too… a girl could do far worse…"

I will myself not to scream. I must make him leave, and quickly, before the poison takes effect. "As I said, my father is not here, Mr. Pratt. It is not a convenient time to pay a call, negotiate payment, or conduct any other business. Please go away and return tomorrow."

"Now, Jessamine – that is not a very hospitable way to speak to our guest."

To my horror, Father strides into the room. He extends his hand to Pratt, who has jumped to his feet. "Tobias Pratt. I heard a man's voice as I was cleaning my boots at the door. I thought it might be yours; I am sorry to discover I am right. I cannot say I am glad to see you, but I concur with what I heard you tell my daughter. We do have unfinished business between us."

He turns to me. "Jessamine, set another place at the table. Mr. Pratt will join us for dinner."

Pratt removes his hat and grins. "Much obliged for the invitation, sir. A true gentleman, you are. In spite of all they say about you!" He guffaws, and my father half smiles.

Ice in my veins, I do as I am told.

I had planned to feign a headache at dinner and drink only tea, but it requires no subterfuge for me to avoid eating with Pratt here. He runs out of ale quickly. He drops his knife and demands a fresh one. He requires second helpings of meat, third helpings of potatoes, followed by more ale.

I fetch and deliver, pour and serve. My own food sits untouched, as it must if I hope to live until morning. But it is torture to keep leaving the table. More than anything I wish to watch my father eat, to let my eyes follow his fork from plate to lips, again and again, as he places bite after bite of my carefully prepared meal in his mouth.

Pratt belches again and loosens his belt. "Don't think this home-cooked dinner will lower my price, Luxton. I know that boy Weed taught you a thing or two. It's time I was compensated, and you know it. Here's what I propose – it's only what's fair. I think you'll agree."

He takes a folded sheet of paper from his breast pocket and passes it to my father. As he stretches across the table he flinches, as if there were a twinge in his side.

Father makes no move toward the paper. "Now

don't be alarmed at the sum." Pratt goes on, a hand to his ribs. "Multiply it by what you'll earn with the potions you learned from the monster, and I think you'll agree..." He flinches again. I count the seconds: one – two – three, until the twinge passes and he exhales.

"Are you all right, Mr. Pratt?" My father speaks calmly, but his eyes follow Pratt's contortions. *Lift the fork to your lips, very good, Father – now one more bite, just one more –*

"Sure, sure. Nothing another swig of ale won't fix. Now, about my money..." Pratt turns pale and groans, clutching his belly. My father puts down his fork. I rise and express concern, and offer to make my special peppermint-ginger tea to settle his digestion.

Take another bite, Father, I think as I fuss over Pratt. *I must keep up this pretence long enough for one – more – bite –*

"Don't trouble yourself, miss," Pratt grunts, doubling over. "My stomach's tougher than a cast-iron kettle. I'm just having a touch of – ow – wind."

As Pratt writhes in pain, my father looks down at his own half-empty plate. At my uneaten food. The blue vein in his forehead goes taut, and he rises to his feet.

"Lord help me!" Pratt yelps, and slips to the floor with a crash. Ignoring him, my father steps toward me.

"Jessamine. What have you done?" Father and I stand frozen, eyes locked, while our dinner guest moans and retches on the stone floor.

"Perhaps… the potatoes were too green." I am in my apron, the scent of cooking still upon me.

Pratt makes a terrible gurgling sound. Father lunges at me with a roar, murder in his eyes. I seize the carving knife from the table and point it at his chest. Remorse is nowhere within me. Instead I feel free, exhilarated at my own daring.

"You wretch! Evil child! After all I have done – "

He grabs at me across the table, but I dodge him easily. Pratt rolls on the floor like a loose barrel on the deck of a ship, nearly knocking Father down.

We circle each other around the table, the deadly

feast laid out between us. I glance down at the plate by Father's chair. He has not eaten nearly as much as Pratt, but he has eaten enough. The full effect will simply take more time. I am glad. It means his suffering will last that much longer.

"Murderess! These poisons were meant for me," he rages.

"As yours were meant for me, Father. And for my mother." I hurl the knife at him and bolt for the door, but Pratt's hulking, unmoored form knocks me to the ground.

The blade has struck Father's arm, cutting a long, shallow gash. He looks down at the wound, his expression one of surprise. Reflexively, he grabs a linen napkin from the table and tries to stanch the flow of blood running down his arm. I laugh. How can I not? He will be dead long before the bleeding has time to weaken him.

He seems to realise it, too. He drops the napkin and wheels toward me. I cringe as he looms above, now holding the knife. In the instant that he raises it to strike, I see it – the change in his colour as the first pain hits.

"No!" he cries, doubling over. The knife clatters to the floor. "No! I – will – not – succumb – "

I snatch the ring of keys from his belt and regain my feet. "Follow me, Father," I taunt from the doorway, in a little girl's voice. "Follow me to the 'pothecary garden, and I will show you which of your beloved plants I used to make your dinner."

"Fiend!" He staggers toward the door. "You do not know – the danger – within – "

"I know more than you could imagine." I race out of the cottage, then turn with deliberate cruelty up the hill. For years Father locked me out of his precious garden, but the poisons are my allies now, not his. The closer I get, the more clearly I hear Oleander's merry, mocking laughter ringing in my ears.

I open the lock and the gate swings open, welcoming. The plants quiver in anticipation at my approach.

By the time he reaches the crest of the hill my father is baying in agony, clutching his belly, gagging on his own bile. Still he follows me through the gate. Once inside, he crumples to the ground. I watch as he drags himself toward me.

"Jessamine, it is not too late… if you tell me what poison you used… I might know a cure…"

"Look it up in your poison diary, Father. Or have you misplaced it? It would certainly be a pity if your precious book were lost."

He looks up at me, wide-eyed. "Have mercy," he gasps. "I am your father."

I gesture around at the inhabitants of his garden of death. "These are your true children. Not me."

He moans, whether in response to my harsh words or to the deadly mixture coursing through him, I cannot say.

"It is not an easy death, is it?" I crouch low, next to him. "I came very close to discovering that myself, thanks to you. Just as my mother did."

"Your mother – did what she did – *willingly* – "

"Then you should be as willing. I know how poison fascinates you. Surely dying from it will fascinate you, too." Leaning closer, I hiss, "It is a pity you cannot take notes."

With that, I leave my father in the dirt to die.

The deadly plants nod and flutter their approval as I pass. Their seductive voices remain out of my hearing, for I do not have Weed's gift. But in my heart I know that they – and their master – are proud of me for what I have done.

I lift my head to the sky, hoping and fearing to catch a glimpse of Oleander's presence.

"I did what you bid me do," I whisper. "Are you pleased?"

A darkness drifts across the sky, and a cool, gentle rain begins to fall on my upturned face.

I lock the gate behind me on my way out.

My work is not yet finished. First I must return to that nightmare parlour to dispose of the poisoned food, for I would not wish a bird or mouse to nibble on it. I step around Pratt's body to do so. He is already dead, pur-ple swollen tongue protruding from his mouth, wild eyes staring into the void.

For a moment, a sick feeling sweeps through me. Even a cretin like Pratt is one of God's creatures, is he not? I did not intend to cause his death; it was an accident born of his own gluttony, but still, his blood is on my hands.

Then I remember how he mistreated Weed, and a great peace fills me. Perhaps this, too, is a kind of justice.

Next I prepare my disguise. I mix fine powders of Punjabi henna and Arabian katam that I find on the shelves in the storeroom, and darken it with indigo from the woad in my dye garden. I prepare a skin cream of crushed walnut shells and oil, and a lip tint of beeswax, dandelion root, and beet juice.

While these cosmetics do their work on my hair and skin, I fill my purse with money. I have plenty, earned by my skill as a healer. I pack what few clothes and other items I imagine I will need. And I decide to bring some powerful herbs from the locked case in Father's study, in case I must defend myself.

I do not bother to search for the right key on his ring. Instead I shatter the glass with a paperweight and take what I please: belladonna, monkshood, snakeweed, moonseed, and more. I wrap each one in parchment and tie it with string.

A raven comes and perches on the windowsill as I make my preparations.

Thank you for your bounty, Oleander, Prince of Poisons, I think. *Thank you for all that Mr. Pratt has already received, and all that my father is receiving still, as the poison twists like bramble in his gut, burns within his brain, presses like a boulder upon his heart.*

I am ready. I see myself in the mirror: myself, and not myself. Father thought I had grown to look like my mother. No more.

I pause for a moment on my way out of the cottage, to say a silent goodbye to my kitchen garden, my cooking herbs and medicinal plants, my teas and dyes. They have served me well, for so many years. I am sorry they will soon be neglected and overgrown.

But that is the way of gardens. Old plants wither,

and new ones sprout. The strongest plants survive at the expense of the weak. Even the most well-tended bed turns to a jungle in a season, without the gardener's restraining hand.

You learn quickly, lovely. I am impressed.

Take me to Weed. I am ready.

Weed is on the move, even now. And so must you be. First you must get away from this place, and let the trail run cold. Unless having dear Crabgrass watch you hang from the gallows is the sort of reunion you envisioned?

A shiver of fear and outrage runs through me. Who would blame me for what I have done, if they knew my father's wickedness?

Your father was not the only wicked man in the world. Now run. Run far. I will tell you when to stop.

But in the end, you will bring me to Weed, won't you?

I always keep my promises, lovely. You ought to know that by now.

5

Deep in the forest is another world, yet three hours on foot brings me back to where the humans dwell – to the site of my worst nightmares, and my happiest memories.

As I descend the familiar paths toward Hulne Abbey, I begin to detect a bitterness in the air, like burning wool. There is another smell, too: the stench of death.

The cottage door opens with a push. Foul smoke pours from within, but I feel no heat from a fire. Covering my mouth with my sleeve, I enter.

Splayed on the floor of the parlour lies the body of my old tormentor, Tobias Pratt. He is dead but has not been for long. A few hours, no more. Already the flies are busy doing their work. The stink is horrid even before rot has had time to set in. Then again, he stank when he was alive.

"I am sorry to see you, Mr. Pratt," I say, pushing his body over with my foot. "But not sorry to see you dead." There are no wounds anywhere, though there is a thin trail of blood leading to the door. Pratt was poisoned. Whose blood it is I dread to think.

I wave away the bitter smoke and quickly find its source. A candle has fallen from the dining table to the carpet, but the stone floor will not burn, and rain has blown in through the open door and wet the carpet's edge. Edged by stone and damp, the fire has smouldered in place.

The silver candlestick that started the fire is now cool enough to touch. It is wrought silver, for special occasions only.

I place it back on the table, and my hand lingers

on the smooth metal. The last time I saw this candlestick was the night of my betrothal to Jessamine. That was the night her father first poisoned her, with a polluted toast that was meant to celebrate our future life together.

I wish he were the one lying here dead, instead of Pratt. If I am lucky I will find his corpse elsewhere in the house.

But what else might I find? The terrible thought goads me on. I pass through the parlour and climb the stairs, until my head is above the worst of the smoke. These stairs lead to the old bell tower that houses Jessamine's bedchamber. Coughing and gagging, I catch just enough breath to race the rest of the way up.

"Jessamine!" Above all I fear to see her sprawled lifeless on the bed. But the room is empty, the bed neatly made. The drawers have been left half open. Some have been emptied. There is no sign of chaos, struggle, or flight. Rather, a calm departure.

"What has happened in this house?" I demand of the morning glory that twines around her window.

"Gone, all gone," it croaks, and can say no more, for the vine is brown and shrivelled, as if from an early frost.

Pratt is dead. Luxton is missing. Jessamine has fled, but with time to prepare for her leave-taking. Evil is afoot, of that there is no doubt. Out of the cottage I run, up the path to the left, until I reach the dreaded gate.

It is locked, but through the iron bars is a sight of desolation. Brown autumn leaves are scattered thickly over the garden, though the trees elsewhere have scarcely begun to change colour. I see shrivelled stems and plants dying back to the ground, as if winter were already here.

I had steeled myself against the sickening power of this place, but it is faint. I reach my hand between the bars and seize the nearest plant, a privet shrub that should still be dense and green. At my touch, the stems crackle, and dry leaves scatter to the ground.

"What happened in that house at the bottom of the path? Do you know?"

The brittle, cackling laughter grates at my

ears. "Poison happened, Master Weed! Surely you understand."

"I understand all too well. But why would Thomas Luxton poison Pratt?"

"Poison happened, not once, but twice."

"Don't speak in riddles. Did Luxton poison the dead man or not?"

"Luxton did, Master Weed. But Thomas Luxton did not."

Not once, but twice. I struggle to make sense of the words. A terrible understanding gathers in me like a storm. "Tell me the truth, quickly: Has Luxton, Thomas Luxton, I mean – has he been poisoned also?"

"Poisoned, poisoned, poisoned!" the skeleton plant singsongs with glee. "He has been very well poisoned indeed."

She had cause, I think in despair, *surely she had cause. But Jessamine? A killer?*

Leaves curl and fall off the privet, one after another. "One more question, Master Weed, for time is short. Winter is coming soon, much sooner than you think – "

"Tell me where Jessamine Luxton is."

"Lovely Jessamine." The privet sighs. "We all admire her, but she is Oleander's prize, and no one else may covet her. He is so proud of her for what she has done! Such a brave and talented girl. A natural, one might say."

"Where is she?" I rage. "Answer, before I rip you up by the roots and throw you in the fire!"

"No more questions, Master Weed. Soon it will be cold, so very cold – "

Furious, I reach both hands through the iron bars, ready to snap this insolent shrub in two. But I am stopped by a sound. A low moan, human, and yet not human. The wind would moan like that, if it could feel pain.

"What a pit of evil this garden is," I mutter. "If I should ever lay eyes on it again, it will be to raze it to the ground."

Again the wind moans, but the leaves on the trees do not move.

The words of the half-withered privet bush fill me

74

with rage. I snap off its brittle limbs at the ground and run back to Luxton's house of death for the last time.

Using the dry branches as kindling, I fan the hearth embers into a blaze, and set fire to anything that will burn. I stand outside at a distance and watch until the flames leap out of the upstairs windows and the air fills with the smell of burning flesh.

One might think that this is some final act of kindness from me toward Tobias Pratt – to let the carcass of my former caretaker burn in the pure flame, and thus deprive the maggots of their meal.

But truly, it is a kindness to the maggots. I would not wish any innocent worms to feast on those vile remains. And if Jessamine had something to do with it, better that the body be destroyed.

I watch the flames dance and light up the night sky. My days in hiding are over. I must find Jessamine and rescue her from the path of evil she has stumbled upon. If Oleander has gained some sway over her, it will be a terrible path indeed. Already it is littered with blood, poison, and death.

I never paid much attention when my old guardian, Friar Bartholomew, would read to me drunkenly from the scriptures, but I heard enough to understand this: Whatever road Oleander has set her upon can lead only to hell.

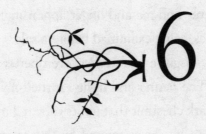

6

I AM ROWAN. I tell myself over and over, in tempo with the steady drumbeat of carthorse hooves slapping against the dirt. *Rowan. Rowan. Rowan.*

Not Jessamine. That name cannot be spoken, not until I am back in Weed's arms and the world has been put right again.

I chose the name Rowan for myself, for I have blood on my hands, as red as the berries of the rowan tree. My new companions accept the name, and me, with no suspicion that I can so far detect, save a kind of wolfish curiosity from the men. I feel it in the way their eyes find me and linger appraisingly, as if I were livestock being examined before a sale.

My disguise has worked even better than I dared hope. The henna and indigo turned my blond hair a rich, dark chestnut that glints ruby red in the sun. My pale skin has been tanned by the cream I prepared. The crimson of my lips owes its tint to the stained beeswax. I look older. Worldly. A woman to be reckoned with.

Only my eyes are the same. They are my own pale eyes, empty of all feeling, ice blue from within my newly tawny face.

They are the same, and yet not. For now they are murderer's eyes. And, may I say, lovely – your eyes have never looked so beautiful.

With the gaze of my fellow travellers upon me, I must struggle not to react outwardly when the demon spirit whispers these sinister thoughts. The true price of my bargain with the Prince of Poisons remains unknown to me. Have I traded my sanity for his aid? My soul for his protection?

If I have, so be it. It is too late for remorse. What has been done cannot be undone. My mother's killer is dead; does it matter that he was my father? And Oleander will keep his promise and deliver me to Weed when the time comes – I believe he will. That is all the salvation I need.

The stage-wagon journeys on, a slow, jolting ride. I close my eyes and feign sleep, for I wish no girlish tears to betray my anxious heart to these strangers who ride with me. I seek no offers of friendship or sympathy. I am the maker of my own dark fate, and I would have it no other way.

Beautiful eyes… murderer's eyes…

My eyes – I remember the night I let Weed anoint these eyes of mine with the dangerous juice of the belladonna berry. I was blinded with passion. So was he. Both of us flirting with madness, yielding to bliss – in truth, much of what happened that night I am unable to remember. The belladonna and tainted absinthe my father served us made sure of that.

I wanted to remember, surely – in the days and

weeks afterward I taxed my imagination feverishly to relive every touch, every wild urge, every vow of love and murmur of desire, until my memories and fantasies were so thoroughly mixed even I could not tell them apart.

Now it is the balm of forgetting that I crave. I begin to see how lucky the plants are, to die and come back each year, all hope and innocence restored. How sweet it would be to bury my pain in the earth and start fresh, like a daffodil in spring.

There is a packet of belladonna berries in my bag, along with many other potent and deadly herbs. It would be tempting to lose myself in some dark, intoxicated bliss – but I must not squander my supplies. Who knows what I might need them for?

The wagon lurches along the southbound road. We left early, in the dark, loading our goods and luggage by torchlight in the Alnwick town square. In time the cool, rosy sky of dawn turned to morning light, and morning light to a blazing noontime.

Now the day grows unseasonably warm, with a strange, clear light – the kind of day that comes only after the passage of a storm. Steam rises from the wet earth. Surely the seventh day of creation would have looked no different than this.

The other passengers shed their wraps and jackets in the unexpected heat. The wise ones have packed food and flasks of water to drink; I have none, nor do I have any wish to eat. I pull my hat low over my face, and hope the sweat I feel gathering beneath the band does not smudge the tinted salve on my forehead.

"A three-legged mule'd hop faster than this rickety crate on wheels. We'll be lucky to make our inn by nine o'clock. What I wouldn't give to be astride my own fine Irish horse! How about you, miss? Are you getting off at Newcastle, or heading further south?"

I dare not remove the hat, but I tip my face up so I can see who speaks. "Did you address me, sir?"

"I surely did. Though you're under no obligation to answer." The man lets out a sharp laugh. "It's going to be a bloody long uncomfortable day, is the point

I'm making. I'm passing the time with friendly conversation." He lowers his voice, as if confessing a crime. "That's the Irish blood in me, I suppose."

He is a well-built man, neither young nor old. Handsome in a rough way, and ruddy faced from a life spent out of doors. I start to offer a vague reply but catch a mouthful of dust and find myself coughing until my eyes water. He watches me, almost amused.

"The road'll get worse as it dries. The fine dirt gets in your nose and lungs. You might want to tie a kerchief over your mouth." His eyes drift down and pause for a moment upon my painted lips. "I was christened Zachariah, but I go by the name of Rye. I'm a horse trader, though at the moment I'm clean out of merchandise. I did well at the St. James Fair this year, for sure; sold four of my fine Irish Draught horses and a half dozen Connemara ponies. Leaving me without a ride home, as you can see. How does your business do for you?"

It takes me a moment to understand his meaning; he assumes I am some sort of merchant, else why would I be travelling with this caravan of trades people? "Well enough," I answer, my voice curt.

He steadies himself against the sway of the wagon by leaning forward and grabbing the rail behind me. It brings his face far closer to mine than I would wish. Our eyes meet, and I see what lies in his: easy pleasure in his own male strength, frank desire, a touch of scorn. "And what kind of wares do you sell?" he asks, a sly taunt in his voice.

Before I can fashion my reply, barks of raunchy laughter explode from a pair of eavesdropping women who ride near us, heaped together with their bundles.

"Nothing you could afford, I am sure," I retort. My intent is to make him leave me alone, but my words are heard by all and become the cause of more laughter.

I fight the anger that rises in me. I wish this man to know what I am capable of – to fear me, even. *Rye, indeed,* I think, *for with one carefully prepared shot of whiskey I could make you suffer. Then you would know the true nature of my wares.*

But even as I think it, I force my rage into hiding.

It is safer to act the part my companions have already chosen for me: the lone woman traveller of haughty bearing, flashy looks, and questionable virtue. It is my aloofness that provokes them. I will have to soften my manner, if I have any hope of getting far without drawing undue attention to myself.

The laughter dies down. My new acquaintance slaps his leg and smirks. "Ah, you're all right, then. What'd you say your name was, lass?"

"Rowan," I answer, risking a tiny smile. "My name is Rowan."

As the day grows long and the horses tire, the men are asked to get out and walk each time the wagon climbs uphill. Late in the afternoon, we sink in a pool of mire that spans the rain-rutted road. Then all of us must climb out and wait until the wheels can be freed from the mud.

I use the time to stretch my legs, and to eavesdrop. I know it is only a matter of time before news of a gruesome double murder spreads through the county. When the dreadful scene at Hulne Abbey is discovered, will anyone suspect the apothecary's quiet, golden-haired daughter of the killings? Or will they assume she was one of the victims? Slain and the body hidden somewhere, or, perhaps worse, abducted?

But among my fellow travellers I hear only talk of trade: the rising cost of goods and travel, and the difficulties posed by highwaymen and other roadside thieves. I learn that my companions include weavers, potters, tinsmiths, and other artisans, as well as a few shadier characters, like Rye. Not only horse traders, but smugglers of black-market salt, tea, and tobacco to the grateful subjects of King George who cannot or will not pay the heavy taxes levied by the crown. It seems these outlaws travel with us not only for their convenience, but for our protection as well – they get free passage and lodging in exchange for the security of their armed presence.

The wagon wheels are freed, the journey resumes, and the afternoon passes in relentless heat and cramped quarters. The deliberate *clip-clop* of unwilling hooves and the grind and squeak of cartwheels on gravelly dirt become our travelling song.

It feels like a kind of purgatory, save that it does eventually come to an end. Just as Rye predicted, it is pitch dark and nearly nine o'clock by the time we reach our inn at Newcastle. A supper waits for us there. At the meal I sit a little way away from the others, with my small tin plate of potatoes and a chunk of unidentifiable meat, long gone cold.

The tastelessness of the food does not matter to me. I eat only to preserve my strength. Now that we are at a public inn, where people come and go and gossip of the region has a chance to spread, I once again find myself eavesdropping. And, like a rare hummingbird that will only sip nectar from one particular kind of flower, my ears are tuned to a single word: *murder... murder... murder...*

So far, nothing. The men ask for gin and argue about politics, Catholics, the French, and the King. The women stick to small ale and trade complaints of bad business and worse husbands. There is no mention of a double killing near Alnwick or of a missing girl. Good.

It has been a long day after a sleepless night, and danger has not found me out – at least not yet. My belly is full, and I treat myself to a glass of ale. I could go up to my bedchamber; I have paid extra to sleep alone. But the heat of the day has given way to a cool night, and I know I will be shivering once I leave this great room with the fire burning in its hearth. Still, my eyes grow weary. If I do not retire soon I will fall asleep in my chair.

"Hello."

I startle, for I seem to have drifted off. Before me stands a girl, a chunk of buttered bread in her hand. For a moment I do not know where I am, or if I am dreaming. She is young and exceedingly pretty, but I have not seen her like before, except in a book of Arabian tales I read as a child: olive skin, eyes black as onyx, and long dark hair that hangs straight as a horse's tail.

The girl holds me in her frank, unblinking stare.

What should I do? The thought of chatting with her as if I were not a murderer, offering the carefully prepared tale of my false self, fills me with the first panic I have felt since leaving Hulne Abbey. I feel caught. Guilty. Where is the remorseless strength of purpose that held me in its grip not twelve hours ago? The innocent gaze of this child has melted it away, just as the frozen lake surface surrenders all its might to spring.

"*Salaam.*" I do not recognise the word, but she says it as if expecting some reply.

It is too late to avoid her. I nod a welcome and move aside on the bench to make room for her to sit. Instead, she stands before me and offers a few sentences of greeting in a strange tongue.

"I am sorry; I do not speak your language." My fear turns to relief. If I am lucky she will not speak my language either, and I will be safe from her attentions.

But she smiles shyly, and answers in perfectly correct, melodically accented English. "Sorry, miss. I thought you might be Persian, like me. I have never met a girl from my country here in England."

She tilts her head and lets her dark hair swing to one side, releasing a faint smell of incense. "The Afghan traders sometimes look like you, too. Brown skin and dark hair with light eyes. Beautiful people! They have many fine rugs, though not as fine as ours. But you are English, then?" She seems disappointed.

"I have some ancestors from Ireland," I say, thinking quickly. "Dark hair and blue eyes are not uncommon in that country."

"Irish? Like Mister Rye. No wonder he likes you. My father says he looks at you like you are a prize Arabian horse, waiting to be broken to harness."

"Really?" I should take offense, but it is a novelty to me, to be seen in such a way by a man. "What else does your father say about him?"

"That he is a smuggler and will hang from a noose someday, if the customs men get him. That, or end up richer than King Croesus." She says it unselfconsciously and lightly touches the skin of my arm, near the wrist. I have tinted every inch of my skin that shows: my face, my neck, and my lower arms, too. "But you do not look like Mister Rye, either. He is red and freckled. You are brown, like me."

"I should have stayed out of the sun." My smile is unforced now, for I see this girl is no threat. She is simply curious, and in need of another young person to talk to. It is hard to be a lone child among preoccupied adults. I know that all too well.

I tug my sleeve down lower on my arm. "Why have I not seen you before? You do not ride in the wagon with the others."

"My family sells rugs." She settles herself on the bench next to me. "We have our own cart that travels behind the big wagon. My mother rides on top of the rugs, and I ride behind my mother. My father rides too, sometimes, but mostly he walks behind the mule, cursing at him to go." She drops her voice low and imitates a man's angry voice, speaking in her own tongue again. Then she giggles. "It is well you cannot understand what I said. It is bad words in my language."

"You are a good mimic. But if you have your own cart, why do you follow us?"

"It is not safe to travel alone on these roads. The rugs we sell are very beautiful. The women of our village weave them. My grandmother ships the finished rugs to us from Tabriz while my parents and I travel and sell, travel and sell. This year they told me to stay home with Maamaan. Learn to weave, be a good girl. But I refused. I want to see the world! And I am good at selling. Better than my father, even he says so," she answers.

Another bite of bread disappears into her mouth. "They take months to weave, these rugs. Twenty shades of dye! Every design tells a story. I would like to show them to you." She says all this with a practised air. I can easily imagine her as a toddling child, praising the merchandise to charmed buyers in a lisping baby's voice.

"Tomorrow morning, when the sun is up, I will be sure to admire your rugs," I promise. "I must warn you, though. I will not buy any, at least not now. I have no need for carpets at present."

"Of course. You need a home first, yes? A home

91

and a husband. Then rugs. Then babies!" She giggles, and her teeth flash white. She cannot be more than eleven or twelve. "Here's what I think, Miss Irish: If you buy the right rug, then the rest will come."

"If your rugs could do all of that, they are certainly worth a lot of money," I agree.

"They are. Four hundred knots in every square inch! My name is Maryam. It is nice to meet you." She presses her hands together and makes a little bow of greeting. Then she holds out the last bit of her bread. "Take it."

I do, and eat it with gratitude. "My name is Rowan," I say. By now I have almost forgotten that it is a lie.

THE JOURNEY SOUTH TAKES on a rhythm of its own. We pack the wagons before dawn, travel all day, and stop at a roadside inn at night. The inns are humble, and I sleep in my clothes to avoid flea bites.

Day by day my false identity has taken shape. I have told those who insist on knowing that my trade is fine embroidery and my finished pieces have all been sold. Now I journey to London to seek work in the dressmakers' shops there.

Where I am truly bound, even I do not know. *Patience*, Oleander whispers in my dreams. *Patience*, *lovely. Do as I say, and all will be as I promised.*

I obey, for what other choice do I have? I act the part of Rowan and put as many miles as I can between myself and my crime. I live for the day when Oleander says I can stop running and leads me to Weed.

In the meanwhile I try to keep to myself as much as I can without seeming standoffish, but I am peppered with questions: How does a young, pretty girl like me dare travel the countryside alone, with so many villains and highwaymen about? Where is my family? Why do I not have a husband? Have I been disinherited? Disgraced?

I just look away sadly, and let them wonder.

At least Rye has let me be. Too restless to sit in the wagon, he has taken to walking alongside the cart horses, and chats amiably with them for long hours at a time. They seem glad for the company, and always keep one ear swivelled in his direction.

Sometimes, after dinner and before I retire to the modest room that is mine for the night, he makes a point to pass by whatever quiet corner I have chosen for myself. He speaks only brief pleasantries, but always brings me some offering: an extra slice of bread, a glass of small ale. The girl Maryam will sit and eat with me on occasion. When she does, he brings a morsel of cake for her as well.

Even these minor attentions do not go unnoticed by the others. This morning, as we boarded the wagon, I overheard one of them, a thin widow named Agnes who sells fine dyed yarns she spins herself, swearing to her companion that I have bewitched the horse trader. The other woman snorted and accused her friend of being jealous.

I cannot travel much longer with this group.

On Saturday we stop for the night at a small inn called the King's Head. By law we cannot travel the roads on Sunday, so there is no need to rise early; we will spend tonight and tomorrow in this town and resume our journey on Monday.

The law is meant to make people devote themselves to worship. Instead, it is an invitation to release all the pent-up boredom of our journey. Once our party has settled at the inn, unloaded our luggage, and dined, the revelry and drink begin.

Monday, I think as I watch the ale being poured. Monday I will part from this group. They will leave before dawn, and I can secure a place in some other inn, under some other name, and plan where to go next.

The carousing promises to last well into the night, as nearly all the members of our group gather, tankards in hand, and pull chairs into a half circle around the fire. First there is a round of jokes, with each person telling one in turn. Then a fresh pouring of drinks, followed by more jokes.

This time around, the humour slants toward the vulgar. When the room erupts with laughter, I see Maryam, her face flushed and giddy, asking for some-one to explain the meaning, as her mother shakes her head and tells her to never mind.

Now one of the tinsmiths leads the group in a comic song about the biggest ram ever sold at the Derby fair – a ram so big his shadow blocks the sun itself. The song has a nonsense refrain that gets louder and wilder each time it is sung:

> *Daddle-i-day, daddle-i-day,*
> *Fal-de-ral, fal-de-ral, daddle-i-day!*

Someone calls for ghost stories, with each story-teller enjoined to share a more terrifying tale than the one before. I wave off my chance to speak, claiming shyness. If they only knew what horrors I could tell! It is better that I say nothing.

After my refusal, it is Maryam's father's turn. "The ghost stories of Persia are much too frightening to repeat here," he says, to hoots of disbelief. "I will tell you a true story instead. Completely true, I assure you. Your own hero, the explorer Marco Polo, saw these things with his own eyes. Have you ever heard of the Hashshashin?"

The word seems to exert some power of its own, for at once the room falls silent. The rug merchant glances at his daughter. Maryam is now half asleep on her mother's shoulder, cheeks flushed from the fire. Quietly he continues. "The Hashshashin was an ancient brotherhood of trained killers. Their victims were kings. Generals. Leaders of men. They killed for power, and power only. Their knives had blades edged with diamonds, and their stealth was like the stealth of a snake. No one could hear them approach. Silent as shadows, their daggers never failed to find their targets."

I try to concentrate on the leaping fire, the glass in my hand – anything but the rug merchant's story that holds everyone else spellbound. "Some say the Hashshashin were taught to kill from birth. Some say they were bred for it. By the use of strange potions, their stealth and ferocity were increased. They lived and trained in a mountaintop fortress of stone, and served a master known only as the Old One."

A pipe is passed around the room. Its smoke has a strange, sweet smell. I try not to breathe it in, but soon my tongue feels thick in my mouth.

Everything seems slowed.

Carefully I put down my glass. I do not like this feeling; it reminds me of when I was ill, a helpless traveller adrift in strange and terrifying seas.

Listen closely, my lovely… Listen, and learn.

"Do these Hashshashin still exist?" one of the younger men asks, a note of admiration in his voice.

"Nobody knows," the rug merchant says. "Some claim they were wiped out centuries ago, destroyed by their enemies. They had many enemies, you may be sure. Others say no: They are still among us, controlling the fate of nations, and just as dangerous as ever."

"And what do you think?"

He leans forward, and the fire sends long shadows flickering across his face. "Does it matter? In every nation, in every century, there are those who would kill for power, no? Even here in England. You call them assassins." He spreads his arms. "No matter what shape or form they take, no matter what they call themselves, these people are the heirs of the

Hashshashin. And there will be no peace on earth as long as such killers exist."

"Hear, hear," someone cries. Glasses are lifted, and there are declarations of assent. The rug seller's story has pleased the group, but it has put them in a sombre mood as well.

By now my limbs are leaden. I force myself to rise and begin to make my way to the stairs.

"Speaking of killers," says one of the women, in the conversation's lull – it is Agnes's friend who speaks, I think – "It was all the talk at the market today. I took a walk over, to see what price yarn fetches in these parts. Anyway, there was a murder in some remote house, outside of Alnwick."

Already I feel somewhat outside myself from the drink and sweet smoke. Surely I can listen and stay calm. At least I should stay long enough to hear what is being said.

"Not at the castle. It was at the old abbey ruins. A man is dead, and a girl is missing. The place was ransacked and half burned to the ground."

Ransacked? Burned? There must have been looters, then – unless the tale has grown wings in the retelling. And they mention only one man dead. That must be Pratt, for who would think to look in the locked garden for a second body?

I cannot help but picture the dreadful scene: Father's corpse is lying there even now, rotting beneath the leaves – not even the ravens dare pick over his poisoned flesh, that work will be left to the worms –

"They say a herbalist and his daughter made their home within the ruins. Imagine that! They must have been odd ducks, both of them, to live in such an eerie place."

"Both dead?"

"They found the body of a man, or what was left of it after the fire. No sign of the girl."

There is some clucking of tongues. A woman interjects, "It's bad enough to rob a man's home and take his life. Must they steal his daughter as well?"

"She's ruined by now, if she's still alive. Poor thing."

"Now, being the wench of a highwayman's not such an awful fate," another woman says. Her speech is slurred with drink. "It wouldn't be boring, at least! And I'll bet the money's good."

A few laugh crudely at this. Soon the group's wild spirits are restored.

"A highwayman, eh? Why not? I'd have a go, if the right robber came along."

"I would too, but only if the thief was handsome. Like Robin Hood!"

"Hear that, men? If you want to please the ladies, a life of crime is your ticket to love. At least with this bunch of hussies, it is!"

More drink, more smoke, more song:

This ram had four legs to walk on, sir,
This ram had four legs to stand,
And every leg he had, sir,
Stood on an acre of land.
Daddle-i-day, daddle-i-day,
Fal-de-ral, fal-de-ral, daddle-i-day.

The din is so loud my head swims; I clutch the bannister for balance. Step by step, I drag myself up the stairs.

The butcher that killed this ram, sir,
Was drowned in the blood,
And the boy that held the pail, sir,
Was carried away in the flood.
Daddle-i-day, daddle-i-day,
Fal-de-ral, fal-de-ral, daddle-i-day.

I too feel carried away in a tide of blood. It takes all my strength to climb the second flight of steps and turn into the dark landing by the door to my room. As I fumble for the key, I see something: a glint of light on metal, lurking in a dark corner. The sight makes me gasp.

The Hashshashin, I think, like a foolish child.

"Hush, Rowan." A strong hand reaches out from the darkness and grips my arm. "It's me."

He steps forward, out of the shadows. It is Rye.

He has some drink in him, I can smell it on his breath, but he seems steady and in full possession of his wits.

"I thought ye might be frightened. All that talk of murder." His brogue is heavier with drink, and the glint of metal comes from a medallion he wears around his neck. I have not seen it before, but the top of his shirt is unbuttoned and the medal hangs low on his chest. It is some Catholic saint, the kind of token that could get a man thrown in prison, or worse.

"You are too kind," I say, glancing around into the hidden corners of the landing. I do not wish anyone to see us speaking alone. "But I am not frightened."

"Maybe you should be."

"Of you?" I look at him, and take in the expressive, mocking mouth, the coarse red-brown stubble on his chin. His shoulders are broad, with arms strong and steady enough to wrestle a spirited stallion or soothe a frightened yearling.

"No, not of me, lass," he says quickly. "I'd wring the neck of any man who'd do wrong by a woman that way. I'm no choirboy to be sure, but I have my principles."

"Of who, then?

"Them." He jerks his head toward the great room downstairs, where the carousing continues. "The widow Agnes has taken to crossing herself when you pass by."

"If you wish to speak to me, come inside," I say quickly, opening the door to my room. Rye slips in behind me. I close the door and bolt it.

I light the candle in the wall sconce nearest the door. The room is small and spare: a cot, a dresser, and a washbasin.

I turn to him. "I am sorry I cannot offer you a chair."

He laughs. "You're not afraid of me at all, then?"

"No." I speak softly, for the walls between the tiny rooms are thin. "In fact, I feel safer with you here."

"'Tis a sweet thing to say." His voice softens, too. "And you are a sweet woman, I think, sweet and warmhearted, underneath that pretty face that never smiles."

"Is that why you've come – to make me smile?" Somehow the words come out sounding like an invitation, but he does not move.

"I came to give you a warning. Be careful of that lot downstairs. I don't like the way they talk. Especially that woman Agnes. She's got her eye on you. She's got mischief planned."

"Thank you," I say, meaning it. "You are a gentleman to tell me so."

He laughs. "Easy, now! I'll not be accused of gallantry. I won't lie; there's another reason I came, too. The truth is, I have a fever, Rowan," he says, and I startle, for I have done nothing to reveal my healing skills to these people.

"What sort of fever?"

"Love, I think." His eyes search mine. "Or its close cousin, anyway."

The room sways again. Is it the drink? The late hour? The dance of candlelight in this tiny, cloistered room? Or is it Rye himself: the way he has sought me out, speaking gently, protectively, making me realise how desperately alone I am?

All I know is that his murmured words and warm-blooded presence have kindled an answering warmth within me. I lift my gaze to his. He sees at once what my eyes reveal; I hear it in the change of his breath.

He makes no step toward me but reaches out with one hand. He smoothes my dark hair away from my face, caresses the rim of my ear, traces the line of my jaw to my chin. Cradling my face in his hand, he brushes the curve of my lower lip gently with the tip of his thumb. As if obeying some unspoken command, my lips part, my pulse quickens. Still he does not move.

All at once, it is I who long to kiss him.

"Who are you, Rowan?" he says. "You're younger than you look, I think."

"I am old enough." I let my hands float up either side of him, skimming his strong arms. Gnarled with muscle, hard as packed earth, skin warm as a wood-stove beneath the rough fabric of his shirtsleeves.

"Old enough for me? I wonder if you are. I wonder why you're running, and what you're running from." He gathers up my hands in his and lifts them up, as if to kiss them. Instead he holds them to the light of the candle. "Old enough to be a liar, anyway. These are no seamstress's hands." He turns my palms upward. "More like a farm girl's. These hands know the feel of dirt, I'd wager. Of good rich earth."

He comes closer still and leans his face down to mine. The slow tenderness of his kiss shocks me, and he pulls away long before I am satisfied.

"You are running, aren't you?"

I stay silent, but my breath comes quick. He smiles.

"Tell me the truth and I'll kiss you again. Are you running from something?"

"Yes."

"From what?" He draws me close. His cheek is rough and hot against my skin. "Did you flee a wicked husband? A crushing debt? A mistress who treated you like a slave?"

"I have done murder," I whisper. I know he will think I lie, but a mask made of truth is often the best disguise. I offer him my upturned, parted mouth, and wait for my reward.

Practised healer that I am, I can feel his temperature rise. But he steps back and gives me a hard, searching look. Then he chuckles. "Did you, now? Can't say I'm surprised. There's something lethal about you, to be sure. Very well, man-killer Rowan. Someday you'll tell me the truth. Sleep well."

He starts to go, but I reach for him and seize the front of his shirt. Wordlessly I fasten the top buttons, to hide the medal he wears.

"Lock the door after I go," he says when I am done. "There are too many drunken rogues in this inn tonight. Including me."

He leaves me then, the feel of his stubble still raw

on my cheek. Obediently I bolt the door and blow the candle out.

That night, I do not dream of Weed.

8

THE NEXT MORNING I awaken early. I have only had a few hours' sleep, yet I feel instantly alert, like a hunted animal.

I light a candle, for it is still scarcely dawn, and wash my face with cold water from the basin. With each icy splash, it is as if I rinse away the memories of Rye's presence here in my tiny room. His voice, his form, his warmth, his kiss – all fade until they are no more than the shadow of a half-remembered dream.

My shame is not so easy to wash away. What

would Weed think if he knew how readily I welcomed Rye's embrace? I am lonely and afraid, yes – but is my devotion so weak that I sought refuge in the arms of the first man who showed a moment's kindness to me?

After committing two murders, you feel shame over one little kiss? Really, lovely, you are very foolish sometimes. But the horse trader is right – it is time to move on. I would not have you rotting in some country jail, waiting for the hangman's scaffold to be built...

Oleander's scorn only deepens my shame. But I will obey. As a hunted deer runs through a stream to make the dogs lose its scent, I too must change course often and step lightly, leaving no trail.

I will gather my things and tell no one of my plan. Tomorrow I will slip away before dawn, and leave word with the driver that I have found other means of transportation, so that no one waits or looks for me. It is best not to offer lies and excuses; I wish to simply disappear.

At nine o'clock I go downstairs to get a boiled egg

and some bread from the kitchen. The inn is quiet, the dining room empty. Perhaps some of the guests have gone to church. No doubt many are still asleep, recovering from last night's revels.

I choose a small table for myself and pour a cup of tea. As I do, two women from our group enter the dining room. One of them yawns widely.

"The crying and moaning kept me up half the night," she complains to her companion. "I hope the child recovers, of course, but I'll tell you, I won't spend another night in the room next door if it's going to be another ordeal like that."

"If the girl's that sick, the rug sellers will have to stay behind tomorrow. Just as well, if you ask me. We'll go faster and safer without them. That mule of theirs is slow as a barge! It makes us easy pickings for the highwaymen."

"Are you still dreaming of Robin Hood, sweeping you off to a life of thievery and romance?" Laughter. They have taken a table not far from me. I slide my wooden chair back and clear my throat.

"Excuse me; I could not help overhearing your remarks." I speak in a rush, before my better judgment can stop me. "Did I understand you to say that the little Persian girl is ill?"

The bleary-eyed woman shrugs. "I only know because I rapped on the door this morning asking them to quiet down. Her mother was all apologies and excuses. She told me the child started burning hot with fever during the night and can scarcely swallow because her throat is so swollen. She claimed her husband was already out looking for a doctor, but they'll not find one who'll come on foot on a Sunday, that's certain." The woman clucks her tongue. "I got a glimpse of the girl. She's sick enough, to be sure. Her cheeks are red as a harlot's."

"I am sorry to hear that." I speak sympathetically, but inwardly I am ablaze with anger. Why Maryam? Why now, when I am packed to leave? If anyone else of our group fell sick, I would walk away from their suffering with a heart of ice.

I could help Maryam, easily. But to betray myself

as a healer now would be too dangerous, especially since the news of the murder at Hulne Abbey has spread. How long before someone remembers that the dead herbalist's daughter also had the skill to heal, and to kill?

Even as I sit there, staring at my cold tea, a war rages inside me. The longer I stay, the more peril I am in. But she is a child, an innocent. Unlike most adults – unlike me – she does not deserve even a moment of pain.

Swollen throat, high fever, scarlet cheeks – the kind of fever she has is one I know to be dangerous. It is also not difficult to cure, if one has the correct herbs on hand, and the knowledge of how to use them.

"In what room are they staying?" I ask it casually.

"Third floor, the last room in the hall." The woman gives me a stern look of warning. "But don't you go visiting there, unless you want to risk coming down with the same fever."

"Lord, no! A catching fever, running through the company. That's the last thing we need," her

115

companion adds. "Best keep away, for the sake of all."

"That is why I ask where they are staying." I add a splash of milk to my cold tea and watch it swirl as I stir, a tiny whirlpool of fate that is about to suck me down into its depths. "I would prefer to avoid them if I can. I have always had a strong fear of illness."

I pretend to drink my tea until the women leave. When the way is clear and there is no one around to observe me, I go at once to the third floor and stand outside the door to the rug sellers' room. Still, I hesitate. *Perhaps the girl is not as sick as those women said,* I tell myself. *Perhaps there is nothing I need do but offer my sympathy.*

Why visit her at all, then? The evil prince croons doubts in my head.

If there is some way I can help her condition without exposing myself, I will.

And what if that is not enough?

My hand hovers in front of the door. Do I dare

knock? Do I dare leave without knocking?

Careful, lovely, the voice of my master warns. *Locked gates are kept locked for a reason. Open them even a crack, and you never know what demons might escape…*

My knock is so faint, it is as if I do not wish it to be heard. Even so, the door opens at once.

"Ibrahim! Has the doctor come?" It is Maryam's mother. She looks worn and exhausted. "Oh… it is you. Miss Rowan." She peers past me, down the empty hall. "I thought it might be my husband."

"No. I am sorry." From where I stand, I see that the family of three shares a room that is scarcely bigger than mine. "I heard Maryam was ill. I came by to learn how she fares."

"Not well." Her mother steps aside. When I see the girl, my heart sinks. Her cheeks look painted scarlet, and the whites of her eyes have taken on a yellow cast. She whimpers every time she swallows.

I cannot stop my hands from doing what they know how to do. They fly to her forehead to check

117

her fever, to her neck to seek a pulse. I bend over and press my ear to her chest to listen to her breathing. "Has she taken any liquids at all?" I ask the mother. "Broth? Tea?"

"I try, but she cries in pain and lets it roll out of her mouth again. Are you a doctor?" Her mother's voice is strangled with hope. "Do they have women doctors in England?"

"No." The situation is grave. The girl's pulse is rapid and weak. Her lungs labour for air. Her skin is dry and scalding hot. With a fever this strong she may soon begin to convulse.

Don't be sad, my lovely. Soon her ordeal will be over. That is good news.

But I could heal her.

You could. You could kill her, too, and end her suffering this instant. Why not do that instead?

Villain! Why would I?

Cure, kill – what difference does it make? Either way, you decide whether she lives or dies. Why should you be the one to choose? Personally I prefer to let nature

take its course. But then, of course, I would.

Oleander's rolling laughter rattles my brain. I close my eyes. Our fates are linked, Maryam's and mine. To help her risks bringing harm upon me, for the word of the murder has spread this far. If I expose myself as a healer, it will not take long for someone to grow suspicious. And if I am caught now, I will never see Weed again. I will have sacrificed two lives and traded my soul for nothing.

What shall I do?

It is a fool's question, of course. For the child is blameless, and I am a killer twice over. And in the battle between innocence and evil, which one always triumphs?

Silly to even ask, my lovely. You know exactly who triumphs.

Not this time, I think.

"I can help Maryam, but you must listen to me carefully," I tell her mother. "I am going to leave, but I will return shortly with some medicine that will help her. While I am gone, go down to the

119

kitchen and fetch a kettle of boiling water and a small glass of gin. If anyone asks why, say you are going to make a toddy for yourself so that you might get some sleep. Tell no one that you spoke to me, or that I was here."

She nods but glances worriedly at Maryam. We both look down at the sick girl. Her eyelids flutter and twitch, but her limbs lie heavy, unmoving. "It is safe to leave her for a few minutes," I say gently. "Right now she does not even know we are here."

After securing her assent, I fairly fly down the stairs to my room on the second floor. Once alone, with the door bolted behind me, I unpack my small bundle of possessions to reveal the precious herbs hidden at its core.

With practised skill I prepare a remedy from the ingredients I have at hand. They are not ideal, but they will do: willow bark and chrysanthemum root to soothe the pain and temper the fever. Wild indigo and tree moss to give her young body the strength to fight the infection in her throat.

I grind the herbs to a fine powder in the small mortar and pestle I carry with me. This will help release their powerful essences, since there is no time to let the tincture steep. Then I wrap the prepared herbs in a clean handkerchief and tie it shut. Into my apron pocket it goes.

How very ill considered this is. I do not approve, lovely. In fact, I object rather strongly.

I know.

By now there are more people up and about the inn. I stroll to the stairs without rushing, keeping my head down, wrapping myself in anonymity like a shroud. My feet mount the stairs with a slow, deliberate rhythm, one after the other.

I wait until the hall is empty, then veer toward the room in which Maryam lies. Her mother has followed my instructions to the letter. Quickly I prepare my potion, mixing the ground herbs with small amounts of gin and hot water. I stir and stir again, doing all I can to persuade the herbs to release their powers into this improvised remedy.

Her mother moves forward to assist as I prop up Maryam on pillows. The girl is groggy and her head wants to loll to one side, but the pain in her throat makes it snap back. Her whimpers rise and fall in her delirium.

Her mother holds the girl's head steady as I spoon the first drops of the mixture into her mouth. The child grimaces and gags, but together we hold her fast so the liquid has no place to go but down her throat.

Slow tears spill from her mother's eyes, but the woman does not say a word. "It is bitter, because of the gin," I explain. "She will not like the taste. But it will help her, I promise you."

"When?"

"Soon. Within a few hours you should see some change. Give her another spoonful, every fifteen minutes, until all the mixture is gone."

She looks at me, afraid yet indomitable. This woman would do anything to save her child. For her sake, as well as Maryam's, I pray this medicine does not come too late.

"You are a healer," she says. "Why did you not say so?"

I shake my head. "Tell no one what I have done."

"Why? Among my people the women healers are much respected. Is it not the same here?"

"Not always, no." I ease Maryam's head down again, so that she can rest until the next dose, but her mother takes over, murmuring the prayers and endearments that will do as much as my medicines to call her daughter back to life.

Silently I take my leave. I walk to the end of the hall and turn onto the landing to descend the stair.

"Miss Rowan?" Agnes stands on the landing; a half dozen others crowd behind. The two women I spoke with at breakfast flank her, wearing smirks of grim satisfaction. Agnes seems preternaturally excited, and her arms hang stiffly in front of her, fingers interlaced around a dark handle. My eyes travel downward to see what she carries.

It is my bag. The one that contains the few items I took with me when I fled Hulne Abbey. Including my collection of powerful, deadly herbs.

"We told you to stay away from the rug seller's room," says one of the women from this morning. "Looks like you didn't listen."

"I will go where I please; it is no business of yours. What are you doing with that bag?" My voice drips with venom. How maddening it is, to see my enemy holding my deadliest weapons in her hands without even knowing what they are!

"We found it in your room, Miss Rowan," Agnes says, looking smug. "You left the door open when you ran out awhile ago. Didn't see us watching, did you? We thought it best to take the opportunity to go in and have a look around, given what we thought you were."

"I am a guest at this inn, just as you are. And you are a thief."

"We didn't find the most common signs, that I'll admit. No pentagrams. No bats' wings. No broomsticks. But we did find this." She gestures with the bag.

"That bag is mine." I reach for it, and find myself seized by each arm.

"Is it, now?" Agnes replies. Over her shoulder she

adds, "Did you hear that, everyone? She admits the bag is hers, and its devilish contents as well. Ingredients for potions and poisons! It seems we have a witch among us after all."

I offer no resistance, for I am no fool; I know any attempt to escape will simply confirm my guilt and guarantee a noose around my neck before sunset.

No doubt I will now be tested in some senseless, dangerous way. The execution of witches is no longer permitted by law, but the hanging of those who pretend to be witches is perfectly acceptable. If I am not found to be one, surely I will be declared the other. Either way, the authorities are hardly going to leap to my defence. They believe in witches too, no matter what the law says.

My captors surround me and keep their hands upon me. One man squeezes my arm so tightly the flesh begins to go numb.

"You need not hold on so fast," I say. "Unless you fear I will fly away."

"Ha ha." He snorts, but he looks worried nonetheless, and does not loosen his grip. Then, as if to console me, he adds, "The river Tyne is not far. It won't be long now."

Small comfort. At least now I know they intend to throw me in the river.

By the time this gruesome parade gets to the banks of the Tyne, the crowd has grown fourfold. How could it not? A giddy mob with a stone-faced young woman held prisoner in the centre, being marched toward the river. No explanation is required; the word practically speaks itself: *witch, witch, witch.* It is a form of entertainment not to be missed.

They lead me to the bank, until I am close enough to see the river below. The water is fast and steely grey. The fine spray from where it hits the unforgiving rocks flies up and pricks my skin like needles of ice.

Agnes, my self-appointed prosecutor, steps forward and addresses me. "Don't stand there staring at us with daggers in your eyes, girl. Your fate is in your own hands, not ours. If your heart is pure, it will be shown to all. And if it is not – repent now, and prepare to meet your maker at the bottom of the Tyne." She glances at the water, a hungry look in her eye. "Now, would you prefer to jump, or be thrown in?"

Am I expected to answer? I could kill them all with the contents of the bag that Agnes swings so proudly by her side. Perhaps someday I will get the chance.

"I would prefer that the lot of you burn in hell," I say calmly.

"Toss her in, then." Agnes signals the command, and my captors seize me again. A man's rough voice trumpets over the crowd.

"You can't throw the wench in like that."

It is Rye, breathless from running. He must have discovered what was happening and chased after us. He strides directly to me, and the other men step back. His expression is blank.

"He's one of the souls she bewitched," I hear Agnes hiss to her followers. "Let's see if the spell is broken now."

Help me, I long to whisper to him, but I can utter

127

no sound. He reaches out as if to touch my face, as he did last night in my room. What an eternity ago that seems! Will he be my protector against this unthinking mob? But how could he be? If he defends me, they will take it as proof he is bewitched, and thus of my guilt.

He takes me by the chin, an almost tender gesture. Slowly he tilts my head back, exposing my throat. Then he seizes the neck of my bodice and tears it in two, with one rough downward pull from neck to waist.

I cry out. I am bare, exposed to the midriff. The crowd whoops in merriment.

I wheel around to shield my nakedness from them and try to gather the shreds of fabric to cover myself. Rye picks me up and flings me over his shoulder so quickly all breath is knocked from me. I would scream, but his hard shoulder digs into my belly and I cannot take in air.

He carries me ten paces upriver, my skin chafing against the coarse canvas of his shirt. "Be quiet and let me help you," he growls in my ear as we walk. "In the water this dress would drown you faster than a mill-stone tied around your neck." At river's edge he drops me carelessly to the ground.

"Stand up, witch!" He yells it for the benefit of the crowd. He lifts me to my feet and spins me to face my accusers. I try to cover myself with my arms, my hair. Then, with a raucous cry, Rye seizes the waist of my skirt from behind and tears it from me. Now I do scream. He steps close behind me and seizes me by the waist, speaking rapidly and quietly so that only I will hear.

"I'm throwing you in where there're no rocks. When I lift you up, take a deep breath and hold it in your lungs. I surely hope you can swim, lass – " His remaining words are lost in the catcalls of the crowd.

Then, with his two strong, rough hands hot against the gooseflesh of my skin, he hoists me into the air, naked and helpless as a newborn filly, and throws me into the cold rushing water below.

Even without the deadly weight of the dress, I sink.

It is a shadowy world, beneath the river's surface. The water is cold and clouded with silt. My hair swirls around me like a veil of seaweed, and my limbs are ghostly in the murk. A dying mermaid, I drift downward, ever further from the air. The dim light of the surface quickly fades from view.

A swaying meadow of eelgrass covers the river's bottom; the long, snaking green tendrils beckon invitingly. The air in my lungs presses outward. Now, as the remaining seconds of my life tick away like a clock, the sum of my days becomes visible to me. I see it all at once, like images painted on a globe that spins before my eyes.

Fleeting, infant memories of my mother. Her soft shape, the feeling of being carried, the comforting smells of milk and bread and fresh-laundered linen.

Me as a little girl, my lower lip trembling in shame, trying not to cry while being scolded by my father. Then me again, older, earnest, curious to know all about this mysterious work of his. I watch myself grow expert in the ways of the garden, while still remaining so ignorant of life.

Then comes Weed, and I tumble into a dream of happiness. So brief and yet so sweet, it seems to erase all that has come before, and blinds me to all that might come after.

And then: Oleander. He is a phantom, a nightmare. Yet it is through him I discover the truth of who I am.

Now, about to die, I begin to understand how terrible this world can be. And I am part of it, not separate from the evil and hurt, but carrying it within me like a sickness –

I warned you, lovely. I told you not to bother with that simpering, sickly child. Now look at you. Like a lotus fighting its way out of the mud. Alas, the mud seems to be winning.

Will she live?

The girl? For another fifty years or so, perhaps. Hardly worth all this trouble.

My chest feels ready to burst. My vision fades to a pinprick of light.

I am Jessamine Luxton, I tell myself. *I have lived, and I have loved, and I have killed. I have taken all the vengeance I need to take. Why must I suffer any more?*

Alive, I am Oleander's slave. Dead, I will burn in hell. I already know which is worse.

Tell Weed I am sorry.

I open my mouth. The stale air races out of me in an urgent stream of bubbles.

Tell him I love him still.

No.

I let the slimy water rush in, filling me up, filling my lungs –

I said no. I have plans for you, important plans, and you are no use to me dead. Rise up now.

Tell him I said goodbye.

Tell him yourself, lovely. When the time comes, the refuge of death will be waiting for you. And so will I – but the time is not now. Not yet.

Like a thousand green ropes, the eelgrass binds

itself around my wrists. I open my mouth wider so that the water can fill me, but the eelgrass gives a sharp pull and then releases me. My puppet arms beat downward, propelling me to the surface.

Against my will, my head rises above the water. I gasp, choking, and sink again, but now my lungs know where the air is. Some animal instinct for survival awakens in my flesh; it takes control of my body and overrules my despair.

Again I surface. This time I stay above long enough to let water run out of my eyes, long enough to see the riverbank. It is not far. Choking, I flail and kick like a dog until within reach of the muddy bank. I grasp at wet tree roots that seem to offer themselves to my hands and pull me from the river's powerful current. With their aid I drag my body up the slope and over the slick, moss-covered rocks.

At last I am over the crest of the bank, on level ground. On hands and knees I rest my forehead on the mud and retch, again and again, as the water rises from my stomach and lungs. Even now I sense the eyes of the crowd watching me, transfixed. No one moves to help.

Finally the spasms cease. Still on all fours, I lift my mud-covered face to my tormentors. A few look disappointed that I am alive. Some seem relieved. Others are agape at the sight of me. My bare, battered form is streaked with muck and algae, like the figurehead of a wrecked ship.

But I refuse to feel shame. Refuse, even, to cover myself. Made strong by defiance, I find the will to climb to my feet. I stand there, swaying, and let the water stream down over my body to the ground.

It is Rye who approaches first, slipping off his coat as he does. He extends it to me from an arm's length.

"She sank. Not a witch, it seems," he announces gruffly, for the benefit of the crowd. "Here, cover yourself, girl. No need to drive the men mad. They'll just end up beating the horses later."

He glances at me, a kind of agony in his eyes. I know he saved my life. I know now, too, that he would do anything for me. Poor fool. He knows nothing of what I truly am. If he is lucky, he will never find out.

"Thank you," I whisper as I reach out to take the coat.

"Wait! Don't cover her, Rye." It is the woman, Agnes. "What has she done to her skin?"

I look down. My arms are still brown, but in uneven patches, as the tint has rubbed off in blotches during my struggles in the water. I know my face and neck must be the same. Wet hair hangs in ebony tendrils over my mottled countenance, but my torso and thighs are the color of ivory, and the sparse hair on my body is flaxen blond.

Even now there is a clear line where the tint begins, above my elbow. There must be another below my collarbone. I cross my dark arms in front of my pale body. They look like they belong to someone else.

"Not a witch, perhaps – but she's not who she says she is, either." Agnes's voice rises with suspicion. "Who are you, girl? And why have you gone to such pains to masquerade as someone else?"

The crowd rushes closer to inspect my disguise,

like a pack of wolves that would tear me to pieces. Rye shields me with his body. He turns to face me, then reaches out and takes my wrist, pulling my arm forward.

With one hand gripping my wrist firmly, he draws the index finger of his other hand down the skin of my dappled forearm, pressing hard. His fingertip leaves a pale path of cream-coloured skin in its wake.

"You should have told me the truth, Rowan." His look is hard, his voice resigned. "Now you'll have to tell them."

THEY DRAG ME BACK to the King's Head and sequester me in one of the private drinking rooms off the main saloon. I still wear Rye's coat; over it is wrapped a coarse blanket someone has tossed around my shoulders. From its rank animal smell, I can guess it belongs to one of the horses stabled here at the inn.

My dress lies in shreds in a heap in the corner. The rest of my belongings are laid out on a table. The women go through them like mercenary relatives fingering the possessions of a newly dead and utterly unloved uncle.

The larger mob has dispersed: no witch, no hanging, and therefore no need to wait around. But Agnes is here, still doggedly seeking a means to cause my downfall. The two women whom I spoke with at breakfast are here as well, and a handful of men, including the innkeeper, who has been summoned as master of this house and final arbiter of my fate.

Rye, my would-be saviour, is gone. It is just as well. I have no shame left to feel, but even so, I would not want to face him now. I am exhausted from my ordeal and cannot summon the strength to feign either fear or distress. Oleander's words – *you are no use to me dead* – have fallen upon me like a frost, and I feel myself going quite still inside, numb and yet full of hatred, even as these idiots argue and assault me with questions that I have no intention of answering.

"Tell us your real name, girl."

"Why have you changed your looks? Who are you hiding from?"

"What were you doing to that sick child?"

"Remember, even to pretend witchcraft is a serious

crime," the innkeeper says heavily, clearly wishing to be elsewhere. "What are we to make of all these?" He gestures to the collection of herbs lined up across the table with the rest of my things. Each variety is neatly tied up in parchment. They are unlabelled, thankfully, for I know each one like an old friend.

"Ask her how much money she swindled from the sick girl's parents," Agnes insists. "No doubt she promised to cast a healing spell, with a magic potion made of carrot tops and herbs for soup."

I draw the blanket around me, for a deadly chill is beginning to seep through my veins. "There was an old woman who lived in my village, years ago," I say, telling the tale I practised in my mind during the long walk back from the river. "If she was a witch I never knew it; I was a small child at the time. She could make a tea that cured headaches. She taught me how to do it as well. To this day I carry some of the mixture with me, as I am prone to them. Headaches, I mean."

Their countenances range from doubt to outright scorn. "When I heard that the child was sick, I felt

139

sorry. I took some of my headache tea to the family's room. I thought it might ease the girl's discomfort; I knew it could not do her any harm. It was all I had to give. I asked for no payment, and received none."

The innkeeper lifts a packet of castor beans, which have been dried and ground to a flour to release the deadly poison within. "What's this, then? Headache tea?"

"Yes. And some ingredients to make cosmetics." *One pinch of what you hold in your hand would end your days on Earth,* I think. Part of me wishes that he might demand a taste – but then I would swing at the end of a rope for sure.

"You're a young, good-looking girl. What do you need a suitcase full of make-up for?"

"To sell at the fairs."

"She told us she did embroidery! See, she is lying. It is all lies," Agnes crows, smelling victory.

"I do embroidery as well. But my eyes are not strong, and there is only so much sewing I can do before the headaches come back. The cosmetics are more profitable, but my customers are often – forgive me for saying it – harlots. It shames me to be acquainted with such people, and I do not boast about that part of my business. However, I need to earn my keep, and those wicked women have money to spend." I glance up, all innocence, and fix Agnes with a look. "It is not easy to make a virtuous living, as I am sure you know."

Some of the men begin to fidget, embarrassed. My lie rings true, as all good lies do. Besides, I suspect there are few among them who can honestly claim to know nothing of harlots.

The innkeeper clears his throat. "All right, the girl makes tea and make-up. I see no harm in that. Will you at least tell us your true name?"

"My name is Rowan, and only Rowan. My family name is disgraced, and I swore long ago never to speak it again."

My accusers begin to argue among themselves.

"Why can't she say her name?"

"Disgraced? Maybe we should call a priest."

"What if she's a nobleman's daughter? If she is, there may be a ransom."

At the word ransom they turn back to me, eyes glittering with greed.

By now the chill from my dousing in the river has taken root in my bones. "I assure you," I say through chattering teeth, "There is no one who would pay a ransom for my life. As far as money goes, I am quite worthless to you."

"Worthless? Hardly. I would give Miss Rowan my whole fortune if she asked me for it."

Maryam's father stands in the doorway, hollow eyed with fatigue. "My daughter's fever has broken." He pushes through the group to where I sit and clasps my icy hands. "Thank you. Thank you for your kindness, miss."

He turns to my accusers. "Since before the sunrise I have walked the streets. Hour after hour, I go from house to house, searching for a doctor. But there is no doctor to be found. My heart feels like a stone. I have failed. I think my daughter will be dead when I return."

He pauses. For a moment the only sound in the room is the sharp clattering of my teeth. "Instead I find her fever is broken. My wife says this lady, Miss Rowan – the one you treat like a criminal – came by and held her hand. Offered some tea. Said a prayer for her health. Did any of you do as much?"

There is no answer save the embarrassed shuffling of feet. He glares at the innkeeper. "If trying to help a sick child is a crime, then arrest me too, for going to fetch a doctor. Arrest my wife, for she has been caring for the girl since midnight."

The innkeeper holds up his hands, as if to stave off the rug seller's mounting anger. "All right, calm down, nobody's been arrested. The fever's broken, you say?"

"Thanks be to God, it has." The rug seller's voice crackles with fury. "And I will say one more thing, sir. If this is the way guests are treated at your inn, then you will soon have no customers. No business! I will speak of it everywhere I go. I will make sure that every traveller from Inverness to Baghdad knows what terrible things happen inside this establishment."

The innkeeper grumbles a few words of excuse,

if not apology. But the spell of accusation is broken. He waves his hands at the group and shoos them out, scolding, "The girl wears make-up and drinks tea, and for that you want me to think she's some kind of sorceress! Troublemakers, away with you! If you weren't leaving in the morning I'd toss you out myself, and never mind how much money you spend at the saloon…"

Maryam's father finds a robe for me. He stays with me as I gather up my possessions – all my money has disappeared, but at least the packets of herbs remain – and helps carry them back to my room.

After he leaves, I wrap myself in every blanket I can find. If I could only get warm, I know I would sleep the sleep of the dead, but I cannot. My body is battered, but my mind whirls, and rest eludes me. Time is wasting, but I am too weak to do what I know I must.

Within the hour Maryam's mother arrives with a mug of hot broth. She wants to feed me as if I were the sick child, but I tell her to leave it on the night-stand. "Your daughter needs you," I say. "Go back to Maryam."

She nods, wringing her hands. "My husband is with her now. But I had to come myself to say this: I am so sorry to hear what they did, Miss Rowan. I want you to know I said nothing, to anyone. I kept my promise. When my husband returned from town, he told me that he heard many people talking about a witch, a young woman, being drowned in the river by a mob. I remembered what you said to me, and I became afraid. I told him to go look for you – I am glad he found you. And now see how you shiver! I am afraid you will be the next one to get sick."

All at once my eyes are so heavy I can scarcely sit up. "It is not your fault," I mumble. "I am grateful for your kindness. If you will forgive me, I must rest."

She nods and moves to the door but lingers there. "I do not understand these people," she says. "We will travel with them no more. And you will not, to be sure. Miss Rowan, promise me you will ride with us?

We have room in the cart. My husband does not mind walking. And this way you will be with us – in case Maryam's fever returns, or in case you need someone to care for you."

"We can talk about it tomorrow." I offer a weak smile. "And I promise to drink the broth."

She goes, and I take a few spoonfuls. The heat of it warms me just enough to crawl into bed and bury myself beneath the quilt.

My last thought as I finally drift into sleep is to marvel that there are still good hearts in the world. Not many. But some.

I am sinking, again. Pulled down this time. Weighed down, as if a large stone is pressed upon my chest.

The plants at the bottom of the river beckon. I peer through the murk at the greenish figures below. It is no swaying meadow of eelgrass waiting for me there, but the plants of my father's apothecary garden.

Moonseed. Larkspur. Dumbcane. Snakeweed.

"Why are you here?" I wonder aloud, confused. "You

do not grow under water."

They bend and twist as if consumed by mocking laughter. Then, to my amazement, they speak.

"Welcome, lovely Jessamine."

"Welcome home – "

I wake from the dream with a gasp.

What sound was it that woke me? I listen, frozen. A quiet click as the door opens. A footstep in the dark.

Someone stands, breathing, quite close, inside my room.

"Don't be afraid. It's me. Rye."

"But – the door – "

He lights the stub of a candle and holds it near his face. I see him now, half smiling in the flickering light.

"I'm not what you'd call a law-abiding citizen, I'm afraid. Locked doors don't tend slow me down."

I struggle to rise, to claw my way up from the depths of the dream, but there are weights pressing on my limbs, I feel buried alive –

"Stay under the quilt. You don't want to catch a chill. Not after today." He kneels at my bedside. "I

147

came to say I'm sorry for what I did. At the river."

"You saved my life. I know that."

"I may have, yes. Still. I don't want you to hate me."

"For saving my life? Perhaps I should."

"Don't talk madness, Rowan." He stops. "Ought I still call you Rowan?"

"It is the name I choose."

"Rowan it'll be, then. Until we christen you with something better." He pauses again. "You left me full of questions. I spent the day looking for answers."

"Did you find any?"

"Perhaps. I heard quite a bit of gossip while I was out. That's the other reason I've come."

Something in his tone frightens me. "What gossip?"

"About that murder near Alnwick." He leans close, and his voice drops so low it seems to come from inside my head. "It seems the cottage belonged to no ordinary herbalist, but a well-known apothecary, a favourite of the Duke's. A man with powerful, dangerous friends. A man who could heal with plants, and do great mischief with them, too. His daughter, they say, was equally skilled."

I am fully awake now.

He puts the candle down on the nightstand. "I even found out the girl's name. A fair-haired beauty, she was, named for a yellow flower – "

I raise myself up. "What do you want from me?"

He lets out a low, soothing whistle, as if calling a wayward horse. "I want nothing, lass, except what you might freely choose to give me."

I shiver uncontrollably now, with fear and a bone-deep cold. Without hesitation or permission, Rye eases himself into the narrow bed and wraps his arms around me. Instinctively my body curves into his warmth, like a sunflower reaching toward the sun.

"The sight of you on that riverbank is not something I'll soon forget," he murmurs into my hair. "Like a siren, you rose from the waters, calling me to the rocks. I've caught you like a fever, Rowan."

"I could cure you of it, quick."

"I doubt that." His lips graze my ear. "Tell me the truth – no, don't flinch, I know better than to ask what you don't want to tell. What I want to know is this: Did you like it when I kissed you last night? No more lies, now."

"Yes," I whisper, ashamed. "I did."

"That's a start, then. Listen carefully. I've a proposition for you. Don't say a word until I'm done."

I stiffen in his arms, but it only makes him hold me closer.

"Come with me," he says. "I've been on the road my whole life, a tinker and a smuggler, always on the run. With you I'd have a reason to stop and savour life's pleasures. But we have to get out of this blasted country and never come back. We can do it, too. I know all the smugglers' ships out of Kent and Cornwall, and I'm owed favours up and down the coast. I've made plenty of money, and never paid a penny in tax. Most of it's hidden away back home. We'll book passage on a cutter, and there'll be no questions asked. With the money I've saved we'll buy a little farm in

County Sligo. Or if that's still too close for comfort, we'll go to America. There's fine land in Virginia, they say, and tobacco's a cash crop. It'll be a simple life, a sweet one, and no more running." He presses his lips to my neck. "Come with me."

"Don't." My voice is sharp. "You think you know who I am, but you do not – if you knew all I have done – "

"I've no need to know, now or later. Once we cross the Irish Sea, it's a new land, a new life. Your troubles won't follow you there, whatever they are. I swear it."

Already the bed is warm from his presence, warm as a sun-baked meadow in the long days of summer.

Tempting, isn't it, lovely?

I am promised to Weed. I want no other.

But surely it is pleasant, to lie in the arms of a man who's actually here? Whose kisses stir you even now, despite your protestations of love for another?

It is – pleasant.

And where was Weed when my lovely Jessamine was jettisoned, left derelict at the fetid bottom of the Tyne? The horse trader was there, ready to save you from peril and buoy you back to life – but Weed? Nowhere to be found. As usual.

"Will you come with me, Rowan?"

Why don't you say yes, lovely?

I cannot. I will not.

Such noble sentiments! Surely you don't believe that Weed is alone this evening?

I know he is faithful to me.

Is he? You may be ignorant of his whereabouts, but I am not. Even now, he is handing a single perfect rose to a blushing young woman. She is beautiful, I must say. In fact, she looks a great deal like you…

Thinking my tears are some show of feeling meant for him, Rye kisses me.

"Will you come, then? Will you?"

Go ahead, lovely. Bestow upon him your tender lies, spread your broken wings of love. Obey me, and I will reward you in the end, as promised. If Weed truly loves you, he will take you back, even slightly soiled. And you know how this kind of thing amuses me…

"Yes." I twine my arms around Rye's neck and draw him to me. "Yes. I will."

Happiness spreads like the break of dawn across Rye's broad, unsuspecting face. "Now seal your promise with a kiss."

He kisses me, and more. He is a grown man, and no stranger to a woman's body. And I am no innocent, to be sure.

Is loneliness a kind of love? Is despair? I do not know, but they open the door to passion nearly as well. Perhaps it is the slow poison trickle of jealousy and doubt that Oleander has fed me, but I am not wholly sorry to surrender. For I have been cold, in every fibre of my being, and Rye warms me. His passion is a furnace that burns my pain to ash.

It is exactly the kind of forgetting I need.

He stirs early, long before dawn, and reaches for me once more.

"When we get to Ireland, I want you to marry me, Rowan," he says, groggy. "Say you will."

153

"I already told you."

"Say it again."

"I will. Go back to sleep." He grunts and rolls on his back.

Time to go now, lovely.

I have no money – how will I pay for my travel?

Check the horse trader's pockets. And make sure he sleeps until the sun is well up; I would not have him give chase.

Silently I slip from the bed and go to my bag of poisons and cures. My heart pounding, I do my work quickly and in silence.

I wait until a gentle snore leaves Rye's mouth slightly open. As the sweet drops slip past his tongue, he stirs. Quickly I seal his mouth by pressing my lips to his. It only takes a moment before his sleepy grumbles turn to murmurs of longing. His hands travel to my waist, and he gathers up my gown with work-roughened fingers.

I kiss him once more – he groans – and abruptly he falls back against the pillow, a dead weight. He will not wake again for hours.

I check his pockets and find a thick wad of notes tied in string, but I cannot bring myself to take it all. I remove one bill and put the rest back.

I should make haste, but I cannot help myself: I take a moment to smooth the thick russet hair and caress his stubbled, unresponsive cheek. Asleep he looks younger, softer. Less the cynical horse smuggler; more the trusting, ardent lover.

When tomorrow comes and he discovers I am gone – but I cannot think of that now. I must run, faster and ever further from myself – but where I am running to, I dare not imagine.

10

IT HAS TAKEN THE better part of this long sea journey, but finally I can stand on the deck of this vessel with no churning in the pit of my belly and no bile rising into the back of my throat.

Still, I am eager to set foot on land again. At sea there are no chattering fields of grass, no nagging trees, no farmland planted with acres of dull, complaining crops. But the algae floats atop the waves like a crimson bedsheet, buzzing like a choir of bees. The din never ends.

Worse than that has been the waiting, for I can

156

accomplish little shipboard. Now the wait is nearly over. Soon I will be able to resume my search for Jessamine. This time, I pray I will succeed.

After I left the burning ruin of Hulne Abbey behind me I ran, from this town to that, staying off the main roads, for I knew I looked like a wild man. Along the way I transformed myself. I stole money and clothes, and paid a barber to rid me of my matted hair and beard.

Soon I joined forces with a travelling mountebank's show, where I performed simple tricks to amuse the crowds and part them from their hard-earned coins. What a sight I was! Even Jessamine would not have recognised me, dressed in my velvet suit, with a white ruffled shirt and pomaded hair. My signature performance was making a cut rose bloom on command. Afterwards I would take a deep bow and hand the flower to whatever golden-haired young woman in the crowd looked most like my lost love.

Following each performance I received letters, on monogrammed stationery and reeking of French perfumes, from women desiring to meet me, to bed me, and sometimes even to marry me. It was my own fault, for making such a spectacle of myself, but I did it for my own ends. As a honeysuckle seduces the bees with its bright colour and strong, sweet scent, I needed to do what I must to draw a paying audience. That I refused all offers of companionship seemed only to add to my appeal.

At night, after my huckstering was done, I would read and reread the sole book in my possession: Thomas Luxton's poison diary. I am not a strong reader, for my education by human standards has been poor. But slowly and by candlelight I mastered its pages, each written in the small, neat scrawl of that despicable man.

The diary describes poisonous brews for every possible use. Some work in an instant, bringing death as swiftly as a club. Others are designed to cause a slow, torturous end that masks itself as illness and takes weeks or months to achieve. Some poisons do not even kill but cause incurable madness instead. Some have the power to leave a man paralysed, but fully alive within the prison of his own flesh.

What need could one man have for so many types of poison? Luxton's methods are revealed within these pages, but his purpose is not. Again and again he bemoans his frustration at having to rediscover wisdom that has been lost. There are lists of places where he believed dangerous knowledge to be hidden, and the names of long-dead poisoners whose secrets he wanted to claim as his own.

Near the end of the diary he begins planning a voyage to the place he says houses the greatest apothecary garden that exists. There is nowhere else on Earth, he writes, where this ancient knowledge of the power of plants is better preserved than at the *Orto botanico di Padova* – the botanic garden at the University of Padua, in Italy.

That is my destination now. For throughout all my travels I have been unable to get any news of Jessamine. I have asked the green things that dwell in every hedgerow and planted acre in England if they have seen her, and they say they have not. I ask if she is Oleander's captive, and what dreadful fate he may be planning for her, and they fall silent.

They fear to tell me what they know, which makes me all the more sure that Jessamine must be in danger. But surely a garden as old and wise as the *Orto botanico* will not be afraid. Surely the Prince of Poisons will have no power there.

My time with the mountebank helped me earn enough money to book passage on this ship. And soon – very soon, I pray – the noble healing plants of Padua will help me find Jessamine.

If they cannot help me, I do not know where else to turn. Jessamine, my gentle love, who taught me compassion for my fellow humans! She has fled, that much is clear, but to where? What drove her to commit murder, not once, but twice? If she has fallen under Oleander's power, then he is a hundred times more my enemy than he was before. Yet I am ashamed to admit: There is a kind of relief within me, to know that even Jessamine might be stained with sin. For I too have killed. I too am damned.

There is much I do not understand about the way humans think of punishment and forgiveness, and what happens to sinners when they die. I wish Jessamine was here to explain it to me, for the plants do not speak of heaven and hell. They speak only of the turning of the seasons and of starting anew each spring. Never despair, they counsel, for the orchard that is barren one season may bear fruit in plenty in the next.

Could Jessamine and I also begin again, in time? I do not know, but as I stand here on the rolling deck of this ship, watching the morning mist burn away and the profile of Venice grow visible at the horizon, I curse the plants for teaching me this way of thinking.

It fills me with the pain of longing. It fills me with the agony of hope.

After we set ashore in Venice, a barge takes me up the Brenta Canal to the port of Padua. Following

Luxton's own instructions, I pass through the ancient city walls, hire a gondola to carry me along the canals to the *Orto botanico*, home to the greatest treasure of knowledge that exists about the powerful plants of this Earth.

Once within sight of the university there is no need for directions, for the garden hums at my approach. I find myself summoned by a chorus of voices, of an immense variety and ordered in a way I have never experienced before. It is a glorious and terrifying noise, fierce and beautiful. The battle song of angels.

The garden is large and in the shape of a circle. The stone walls that curve around its edge are white as bleached bone. With my head bowed, I walk along the outside, passing one gate after another, trying to quiet my racing heart.

There is a large fountain at the eastern gate. I pause there, for the mist of cool water soothes me. Already I can sense the mood of this place, so different than Thomas Luxton's garden of terror. The plants within these curved walls are just as powerful, but this garden wishes only to heal.

Cleansed and refreshed by the fountain, at last I am deemed ready. The invitation comes, a swelling song of nonsense words that bids me enter:

Ba lee oh nee

I take a deep breath, for courage, and step through the gate.

Inside is a world of order, of geometry, of balance. The plants nod to me like old friends, and sing their soaring tune, as if it were the answer to every question I might ask:

Ba lee oh nee

I lose myself in the ordered paths. I have come a long and dangerous way to discover what I must know, but now that I am here I feel swept up in the grace and the power of this place, and do not know where to begin.

"Please," I whisper to a bed of violets. "I need your help."

Ba lee oh nee, they sing.

163

"My dearest love is missing – her name is Jessamine. Will you help me find her?"

Ba lee oh nee

Overcome, I sink to the ground. What will I have to do to win the trust of this garden and secure its aid? I lay my cheek on the damp earth of the garden beds, and close my eyes to listen to its chime of welcome.

Ba lee oh nee

Ba lee oh nee

"You! Get up! What are you doing here?"

My eyes fly open, and I see someone – a woman, but dressed in boots, trousers, and a leather apron, as if she were a man. She wears a broad-brimmed hat against the sun, holds a spade in her hand like a weapon, and carries a reed basket full of cuttings. Her face is smeared with dirt.

"I said get up. This is no place to have a nap. You university students will be the death of me." She leans forward and sniffs. "Are you drunk?"

I clamber to my feet. "No, ma'am."

She looks at me with suspicion. "Are you sure?

The medical students are the worst. First they get drunk on wine. Then they spend the night robbing graves, digging up bodies for their anatomy classes. After that they get drunk again, although I can't say I blame them. At dawn they come soak their heads in my fountains to sober up before classes begin. Every morning I find them littering the path like weeds."

I cannot help it; I smile.

"Do you find my story amusing? Because I certainly do not."

"You said the students lie in the path like weeds. Weed is my name. I know it is unusual." I can tell she is angry with me, but I like her, although I cannot say why. "I swear to you: I am not drunk, nor am I a grave robber."

"Your name is Weed?" She laughs, a free, rolling laugh from the belly. "That would be a terrible name for a gardener. I hope you did not come here looking for a job."

"I came here to learn," I say simply. "But I will do

any work you need me to do."

She shakes her head and starts to walk away. "No, no, no, I do not have time to teach every ne'er-do-well that wanders through the gates! The work we do here at the *Orto botanico* is nothing like what you need to know to tend your little farm in wherever it is... Fine! You want to learn? Signora Baglioni will teach you." She points up. "Sun." She points toward the fountain. "Water." She points down. "Dirt. Now you know more than nine out of ten gardeners do. You can open a school if you wish! If you will excuse me, I have work to do, so leave me alone."

She walks away, swinging her spade.

Baglioni, the garden urges. *Baglioni!*

I pursue her. "Signora Baglioni, wait! I am not nine out of ten. In fact, I fear I may be one of a kind. Please – I will show you."

Thinking I might use my tricks to impress her, I run ahead and find a small rosebush, still finishing its autumn bloom. As Signora Baglioni tries to get past me, I cup my hand around a single arching stem that houses a modest bud on the end. Eyes half closed, I murmur.

Excuse me?

Yes?

Would it be possible for you to bloom for me? I would consider it a great favour.

Of course.

As Signora Baglioni watches, the bud grows and swells, until it bursts open to reveal an exquisite pink rose, as dense with petals as a tiny cabbage and as fragrant as a field of lavender.

Signora Baglioni gasps. Then her eyes narrow. "What did you do? Was that some sort of magician's trick? An illusion? But no," she mutters, inspecting the newly opened blossom. "I know this bud was here, I have been watching it for two weeks – and it was not nearly ready to open, not for another four or five days…"

She plants the spade in the ground and leans on it, fixing me with a hard stare. "All right, Signor Weed.

Tell me how you did that. And I warn you, I have no patience for any kind of game."

I shrug. "I will teach you what I know – if you will teach me what you know."

She opens her mouth, no doubt to scold me for my brazenness. But I hear, as she cannot, the reaction of the rose.

Only for you will I bloom thus, Master Weed. Perhaps you will bloom for me someday?

I hold back the answering smile from my face, but not before Madame Baglioni has seen it. She looks at the rose, then at me.

"Very well. Come with me." Her tone is changed. She is no longer irritated, but now sounds almost eager, and full of curiosity. "You will accompany me to my house. We will eat some good cheese and bread and late tomatoes from my garden. You will explain your-self, and I will listen." She glances once more at the rose. "And then, *if* I think you are being completely truthful with me, perhaps I can tell you whatever it is you wish to know."

She walks away without a backward glance, toward the eastern gate. I wait until she is a few paces ahead before I turn back to the rose.

Thank you, I say. Then I follow the signora.

11

The courtyard of Signora Baglioni's house is filled with weathered terra-cotta pots in all shapes and sizes, each overflowing with herbs. The trellised walls are overgrown with moonflower vines, morning glories, and flowering sweet pea. Ripened grapes dangle from the pergola overhead.

As she passes through this miniature paradise, she coos praise, pinches back leggy stems, and deadheads spent blooms with a care and respect I have rarely seen before. The potted plants know I am here; I hear them murmur at my arrival, but all their attention – and devotion – is directed at her.

"Sit. I will bring us something to eat." She gestures to the pair of wrought-iron chairs that flank a small circular table in the shade of the pergola. "And try not to make anything bloom while I am gone. I would be sorry to miss it." She disappears into her house. Soon I hear the soft clatter of dishes and the even *thud-thud-thud* of a knife against a chopping board.

I sit and enjoy the low welcoming hum of the garden. The grapes offer me their sweetest fruit, and I gratefully accept. I cup my hands beneath the nearest cluster. One by one, a half-dozen juicy purple treats fall into my waiting grasp.

"Thank you," I say, biting into one. I hear a sound and look up. Signora Baglioni stands in the doorway, holding a tray, watching me.

"You are welcome, Signor Weed," she says warily. "Unless you were speaking to the grapes?"

Do I dare explain? At least she does not seem afraid of me. She walks to the table and puts down the tray. She has brought two plates and two glasses,

171

a pitcher of wine, a platter of bread and cheese, and a bowl of oranges, figs, and grapes.

"I am sorry," I say, flustered. "I should not have picked the fruit without being invited to do so."

"But you did not pick them. They fell into your hands. Am I right? Here, have more." She offers me fruit from the bowl. Uneasily, I accept.

Is this why the garden urged me to speak to her – because she already knows what I am? Is it possible that this blunt woman in the muddy boots and patched trousers knows more about my "gift" than I do?

She seems to sense my discomfort. "Weed, you say you have come here to learn," she says gently as she sits across from me. "Yet your trick with the rosebud… the way my grapes offer themselves to you, practically leaping into your hand…it seems clear that there is much you could teach me as well."

She tears the bread with her hands and puts a piece on my dish. "But you have just arrived, after a long and exhausting journey, yes? I hear the sound of England in your voice. I should not demand all your

172

secrets before you have even had a chance to eat."

"You are very kind," I say.

She pours wine for us both and pushes a glass toward me. "Still, you have come to the right place. The University of Padua is home to the greatest scholars in Europe. No matter what you desire to learn, there will be some professor here who will be able to teach you. Classes have already begun, but perhaps you can study privately for now, and enroll for next term."

"I did not come to enroll in classes," I say. "You are the person I must learn from."

"Me? I am not a professor." Her voice is sharp. "I do not take students."

"Your name is Baglioni?"

She nods.

"Then I am sure."

"Who told you to seek me out?"

Trust her, the grapevine whispers to me. I take a breath. A lifetime of being called a freak does not make it easy for me to trust any human.

"I did not seek you," I say carefully. "I sought the *Orto botanico*. I came here from England to see it."

Trust her, you must —

Signora Baglioni gazes at me with an open expression, listening. I take another, deeper breath before going on. "Once I arrived, the garden itself told me your name."

"The *garden* told you?"

I hesitate. "Yes. The great round garden. Where you found me lying on the ground."

My words are met with silence, save for the contented buzz of slim honeybees enjoying the blooms of the potted herbs.

"Interesting," she says at last. She spears a chunk of cheese with a knife and moves it onto her plate. "And how did you hear of the *Orto botanico*?"

"I read of it in a book."

"What book?"

The pots of marigolds flanking the door nod and sway, their bright orange heads a field of affirming suns.

Show her show her show her.

I reach into my satchel and remove Luxton's diary.

"This one." I lay it on the table. Its dark leather cover seems to absorb the light. "It was written by an apothecary named Thomas Luxton. The book is beyond evil, but Luxton's daughter, Jessamine, is beloved to me. She is missing, and I fear for her safety. I came to Padua because I hoped the garden could help me find her."

"And the garden told you to come – to me?" She sounds incredulous.

"Yes."

She takes the diary, and opens it. "*Madonna,*" she breathes, and begins to read.

Perhaps it is my weariness from the journey, or the soothing effect of the wine, but I cannot stay awake. I stretch out on one of the long benches in the courtyard, on weathered grey wood that is warmed from the sun, and allow myself to doze.

Now and then I open my eyes to watch Signora

Baglioni read. She goes slowly, methodically. I hear her mutter at points, but she flinches at nothing, and stays fixed on the book. At times she nods, as if recognising some bit of information.

Perhaps this is why I can rest now, I think, settling into sleep at last. *Finally, I am no longer alone in this.*

"Weed. Wake up."

Gently but firmly, the signora rouses me from my sleep. I open my eyes. She has pulled her chair near the bench where I lie. The sun has moved low in the sky, and the diary is in her lap, open to the final page.

"I read it all, every word." Her face is grim. "I confess, I have never heard of this man Luxton. But it seems I should have. This terrible garden of his – *un incubo!* A nightmare. Nothing good can come of it. Where is he now?"

I sit up and stretch my stiff limbs. "Dead. Before I left England, I went to his house. There was another man there, dead of poison. I did not see Luxton, but I was told – the deadly garden itself told me – that he too had been poisoned." I pause, for I do not wish to name Jessamine as the killer. "And his daughter was gone."

"Jessamine? I read of her in the diary. He did terrible things to her. He knew the two of you were in love."

"We are in love," I insist, but my bitterness cannot be hidden.

Signora Baglioni gazes at me searchingly. "If you took vengeance against him, I would not blame you. But it is best if you tell me the truth, Weed."

"I did not kill him," I say, meeting her gaze. "But I wish I had. Signora, the plants of your garden are wise. If they say you can help me find Jessamine, I know they must be right. Do you know where she is?"

"Poor Jessamine," she murmurs. "If I am the one who can help you find her, then she must be in great danger indeed."

She looks as if she would say more. Instead she shuts the diary with a snap. "Earlier I said I wanted to know your secrets. I see now that I must reveal mine. Do you wish to hear them? I warn you, there is great responsibility attached to this knowledge."

I nod.

"Good." Her voice is low and urgent. "Officially I work for the university as the caretaker of the *Orto botanico*. It was planted here centuries ago by great scholars, for a serious and noble purpose. It was meant to be a place where humans could grow and study medicinal plants and try to determine their properties."

She leans back in her chair. The light filtering through the pergola makes patterns of light and dark on her face. "Unofficially, but even more importantly, I am the guardian of a special collection of books and artifacts owned by the university. Some are quite ancient; all are rare. Few people know it exists. This Thomas Luxton seems to have discovered it; he alludes to it in these pages. I wish I knew how he learned of it."

Her face is in shade now, and she removes the hat that has shielded her eyes from the sun. "My grandfather was a professor at the university and a famous botanist. The *Orto botanico* was his responsibility, and the collection was, too. It was he who ultimately realised the danger it held and moved it from the university library to a more secret location." Her eyes flit to the house. I nod, understanding.

"After my grandfather died, my father continued to add to and guard the collection. I have followed in his footsteps, and have made some recent valuable acquisitions. Perhaps none as valuable as this, however." She lays a hand on Luxton's book. "There is much to know. And much, alas, to fear." She stands, and beckons me to follow. "I will show you. Bring the diary with you, please; it should not be left unattended."

"You can have it, if you find it valuable." I stand, but cannot bring myself to move. "Why do you say Jessamine must be in great danger? What kind of danger?"

Gently she takes my arm. "That is what I am about to show you. Swear that you will use this knowledge for good, Weed. Swear it on your life and all you hold sacred. If I discover you don't mean it, believe me,

I myself have many ways to prevent you from doing harm. And I will not hesitate to use them."

"I swear," I say with feeling. "Thomas Luxton was my enemy. His work makes a mockery of nature's bounty. I wish only to find Jessamine and secure her safety. I fear she has fallen into the hands of one who is evil – a greater evil than her father was."

Suddenly the plants of the courtyard begin keening with anxiety. They do not wish me to speak Oleander's name.

"I would like to hear more about this greater evil," Signora Baglioni replies, leading me to the house. She nods at the marigolds that guard her door. "For protection," she explains. "Italian folklore says that marigolds have the power to turn back the evil eye. Do you find that idea foolish?"

"No."

"It is unscientific, perhaps." She shrugs. "But what harm could it do? And we need all the protection we can get."

The house is small and bright, and filled with the aroma of fresh herbs, but we move away from the light and pass through a small door that leads down to the cellar. The stairwell is so low I must duck my head to get through. Not until we reach the bottom can I stand upright. It is not musty and damp, as most cellars are, but clean and dry. There is a faint, not unpleasant smell of fermented grapes.

"It was a winemaking cellar once." Signora holds a candle to light our way. "The grape press was there, and along that wall were stacked the oak barrels in which the wine was aged. When the collection was moved down here for safety, my grandfather made sure the cellar was enlarged and improved. Vents were put in to keep the air fresh. Lamps were added – as were many locked doors." She emits a sharp laugh. "It is a safe place to store valuables, to be sure. Like the vault of King Midas."

Holding a large ring of keys, she leads me through an underground labyrinth, unlocking one door after another and locking them again behind us as we pass. "Almost there," she says quietly, although there is no one to overhear. She fits a key into a shining metal lock, and the final, massive door opens. Signora Baglioni lights all the lamps in the room, until the windowless underground chamber is as bright as day.

The room is larger than would seem possible from the scale of the house. The walls are lined with books and glass cases holding objects that are strange to me – small, full-bellied figurines, dried leaves and nuts, detailed drawings of plants, and other items I cannot guess the purpose of.

Signora Baglioni gestures at the shelves. "Some of these books are scientific diaries, too, though none have the murderous intention of Mr. Luxton's. As for the rest of the items, they come from around the world. Some are thousands of years old."

"Thomas Luxton longed to see books like these," I say, gazing at their weathered spines.

"According to his diary he worked hard and without scruple to discover what he could on his own. Of course, in principle I have no objection to using human subjects, as long as they are already dead," she adds. "Have you heard of the anatomy theatre? It is where the medical school's dissections are performed. They use bears, monkeys, dogs, and human corpses too, when the weather is cool enough. The students have been known to kidnap a body the night before its dissection, dress it up, and take it for a gondola ride down the canal."

She shakes her head in disapproval, but seems amused also. "As I said, the knowledge here spans centuries and continents. But there is a common thread that runs through it all, which is this: There can be no life on earth without plants. They provide food for our bellies and the bellies of our livestock. Without them we starve. Plants also have the power to heal and to kill. But they are more than simply tools for our use. They are alive. Many cultures believe that plants have souls. Some worshipped them as gods. In our own time, in this world, this has largely been forgotten. But not completely."

She waits and looks at me, giving me the chance

to respond. I sense that she wishes me to add something to her story, to reveal what she already suspects I know, or am. But I say nothing, for I am hungry to hear her explain myself to me.

Signora keeps talking, leading me from case to case as she speaks.

"The island natives of the Indian Ocean think the first man – he whom we call Adam – emerged from inside a bamboo stalk, like this one. See this illustration? It is Asvattha, the tree of the universe. The ancient books of India, the Upanishads, call it the foundation of our world. Many other cultures have similar stories about a tree of life. Here, come look at this."

She walks ahead of me to the next display case and points to its contents: a leather bag with a long strap, sewn together with thin strips of animal hide and adorned with painted emblems, seashells, and feathers.

"What is it?"

"One of my recent acquisitions. It is called a

medicine bag, from one of the native tribes of North America. A fascinating people, highly skilled in the use of plants' power. They too understand nature's essence as divine. So much so that they do not think it is man's place to own the land at all. Imagine that – think of all the wars we would have missed!"

Puzzled, I ask, "Is that why this information must be kept secret?"

"It is heresy, Weed," she explains. "We live in strange times. The end of the century approaches, and the people are afraid: What unknown future lies in wait? Everywhere the world is changing. A spirit of revolution spreads like fire. Your American colonies have already succumbed. Now France has fallen prey to it. Some say England will be next."

I squeeze my eyes shut, but I cannot block the memory of the preacher at the crossroads, my hands wrapped around his neck as he pleads for his life – *Repent, for the end is near* –

Her voice calls me back from the past. "The idea that we humans are not the rightful rulers of this

earth, but merely one type of thinking, feeling creature among many, all equally ensouled – it changes
the very idea of what it means to be human. There is
a chemist working in your country, a Dr. Priestley. I
follow his work carefully. His experiments suggest that
plants may even manufacture the air we breathe."

She throws her arms wide. "Plants make the air!
Do you understand what that means? Our food, our
air, our very lives come from the plants. How could
they not be of divine origin, of divine intelligence?
How can we deny that, in some essential way, they are
no less than you or I?"

I thought I would feel comforted to hear her say
aloud these truths that have been unspeakable my
whole life. Instead I become afraid. Why are the plants
so afraid of Oleander that they cannot even speak of
him, or hear his name uttered?

"What of Jessamine?" I ask.

"The collection also teaches us that nature is not
an angel," Signora Baglioni says quietly. "There is a
dark side. Nature has its devils, too: the volcanoes

that spew ash into the sky and blot out the sun, the floods that clear away all life and force the world to start over. The Shinto priests of Japan would say, 'The gentle breeze that cools us in summer is also the hurricane that destroys.'"

"The plant that cures also kills." I close my eyes and feel the cold shadow of the dark prince pass over me. "All is balance."

She takes out her ring of keys and begins unlocking one of the cases. "Yes. There is a balance, and that balance can be destroyed. May I have Mr. Luxton's diary, please?" I hand it over, glad to be rid of the vile object. She finds a place for it on a shelf. "I will catalogue it tomorrow. For now, I simply wish it to be locked away, where no one can find it."

She pockets her keys and turns to me. "As I sat in my lovely garden, reading this book of horrors while you slept, I thought: Here in Padua the air is gentle and the bees hum with joy, but in some windswept corner of northern England, a man with evil in his heart has created a terrible garden that has somehow upset the balance of nature, and let the hurricane have dominion over the breeze, the tidal wave over the gentle swells. Am I right, Weed? Is this the greater evil you speak of?"

I nod. "The poison garden has taken form and shape. It has anointed a leader. He fancies himself a prince."

"Does this prince have a name?"

"His name is Oleander. He calls himself the Prince of Poisons."

She takes me by my arms, searches my face. "And who are you, Weed? What role do you play in all this?"

"I – I do not know."

"You do!" She grips my flesh hard. "Who do the plants say you are?"

I suddenly have the urge to bolt, to climb and claw my way above ground. But the signora holds me fast. "The plants in the forest of Northumberland call me the Human Who Hears."

"And you *can* hear them." She says it with awe. "You hear them all: the trees, the flowers – all the healing plants?"

"The poisons, too."

She releases me. "How wonderful! It is a miracle, surely."

"It feels a curse to me."

"No, no! Listen to the ancients." She gestures around the room. "In all of these lands, the person who could bridge the worlds was revered. He was a shaman, a holy person. Think of it: Humans can survive without animals, and animals without humans, but the Earth itself and all that lives upon it would die a barren, airless death without plants. They are our true masters, though we pretend otherwise. You are an emissary, Weed. A peacemaker, perhaps."

"But what am I to do?" I say, feeling hollow.

"That is what you and I must discover, together. This Oleander is the real danger. Like the Hebrew *golem* of old, he is a monster that rises from the dirt and forgets he is only made of mud."

"Oleander is a monster," I say heatedly. "I would destroy him if I knew how."

She reaches and chooses a book off the shelf. "My

grandfather wrote of just such beings – for Oleander is not the first dark spirit to rise up this way, and will not be the last. Here, listen." She turns the yellowed pages, and reads:

"There is a force of growth and a force of decay, locked in an eternal dance. The force of growth is called Eros, and it is love. And the force of decay is that which the Greeks called Thanatos, Death the Healer, who delivers living beings from their suffering.

"And what if the Prince of Decay should move on his own, and try to seize dominion of the Earth? He can try, but he will fail, for alone he is barren. As the pistil requires the stamen, he needs a partner, an opposite. He must add a force of healing to his killing, a force of light to his darkness, a force of growth to his corrosion. Then his power is complete. Then the Earth shakes, the mountains burst into fire and smoke, the great floods wash away even the strongest arks, and winter comes and does not leave."

"Jessamine!" My fists are clenched; I wish to strike and strike again – but my enemy is not here. "She is a healer. She is light and growth. That is why he has taken her."

Signora Baglioni looks grim. "It is what I fear, too. Jessamine may well be the key to his power. You must find her, Weed – not just for your own sake and hers, but for the sake of us all." A wave of grief crosses her face. "I hope – I pray – it is not too late."

# 12

Jessamine Luxton.

Jessamine Luxton.

The name is so familiar to me.

Sometimes I think the name was once mine. I can close my eyes and conjure such sweet, simple scenes: a girl and a boy, lying together in the meadow grass of a sheep-dotted field. Gazing into each other's eyes, fingers entwined. Two children, playing at love.

The girl's name is Jessamine. The boy – what a strange name he has! It skitters along my memory like a dragonfly on a pond, so close to the surface, never landing. But it is a strange name, of that I am almost sure.

Or perhaps the sweet scene in the meadow is a fantasy, and the story of a girl called Jessamine and the beautiful boy she loves with her whole innocent heart is no more than a dream I once had – a dream I have long since woken from and that is now almost completely forgotten.

For that is what happens to dreams. One wakes, the fantasies of the night fade, and the hard, cold truth of the day comes crushing down until it aches to draw breath.

How it aches, sometimes! A stabbing that tears my heart in two. Enough. Dream or memory, it does not matter. Jessamine is no more.

And what of Rowan, the unsmiling seamstress? In my mind she lies a corpse, bloated and pale, drowned at the bottom of the Tyne. Her naked body is tangled in the eelgrass of the riverbed. Her hair floats in the current; her eyes stare blindly into the murk. Her youthful flesh is blue and cold, food for the crabs and the fish.

Or is it? For I think I was Rowan, for a time. Can she be dead if I live? My mind is very unclear of late. A jumble of thoughts travel in endless spirals, whirling around and sinking ever downward – the past gets buried deeper every day, but I can still remember the warmth of Rye's breath in my ear, and the touch of his rough hands upon my skin.

I rarely feel pity anymore, or any soft or tender feeling, but I feel pity for Rye. He will not trust a woman again, that I know. He will spend his life as he was meant to spend it: as an outlaw and a profiteer, alone save for the parade of naive girls to be wooed, bedded, and cruelly tossed aside. Each conquest will serve as another useless revenge upon me, until in time he forgets me, too – just as I have already forgotten myself.

Belladonna is my name now. It suits me; at least it suits the girl who looks back at me from the mirror. My skin is pale as a snowdrift, for I cannot bear to go out in the sun, and I rarely have the urge to eat. Thanks to fresh applications of indigo and henna, my hair is a lustrous raven black. It cascades like waves of a midnight sea over my angled, bloodless cheeks.

My eyes are nearly black, too – my pupils stare from within a thin ring of ice blue, dark and round and shining, like the deadly nightshade berries I once tended like a mother.

Belladonna. A most deadly nightshade, indeed.

Remember, Jessamine, you will be raising a litter of assassins…

Memory, or dream? A man spoke those words to me, long ago. A stern, forbidding man. He often scolded me. I was afraid of him; that much I do recall.

Was he my father?

My mind goes weirdly blank at the thought. I remember only this: that I left Rye in the dark of early morning, with Oleander urging me on and on.

Run, lovely, he told me, in that mocking voice that slithers hourly within my brain. *Run, though you have nowhere to go.*

I have only enough money for a day's bread – why did I not take more?

195

You should have listened to me, when I told you to let the girl die. Now you will run until you tire, until you hunger and thirst, until your feet bleed, until the snows come.

I will find refuge somewhere – surely someone will have pity on me –

For a time, perhaps. But it will make no difference. No matter where you go, it will be the same as it was with these ignorant, witch-hunting fools. You will be hated, hunted down, despoiled, and driven away.

What shall I do, then?

Obey me from now on, lovely. Obey me without question. I will tell you what to do.

I would not have survived without Oleander. He guided me from one town to the next. When I ran out of money, he taught me how to get more, so that I might buy what I needed to live – clothes, food, lodging, transportation.

From Oleander I learned that when one is skilled in the use of poisons, there is always someone willing to pay for the quiet disappearance of a rival, the death of a brutal husband, or the tragic, fatal illness of a sibling whose inheritance one covets.

I had no idea how easy it would be, to earn money this way. But once one is without hope or scruple, many things become possible.

Yes, once one has ripped all mercy from one's heart, as if mercy were no more than a weed – a straggly weed, to be pulled up by the roots and thrown away with the rubbish! – so many utterly dreadful things become possible.

And truly, it is so difficult to obtain justice in this world. There are days I feel like a healer, still, when I am able to achieve what the law cannot. So I would not call myself unhappy, far from it. After seeing much of England, I have finally arrived in London. I have made many new acquaintances here, and they in turn have introduced me to all manner of pleasures.

Laudanum, for example. The formula is simple. It is made from opium, harvested from the seed case of the poppy flower and then mixed with alcohol. At first I was reluctant to drink it, but Oleander bid me do so, and I soon understood why. It creates the most delicious feeling in the brain. It sharpens my senses like an arrow, until the world and its wonders are made vivid beyond words.

Laudanum makes the bright, clean scent of the night into an intoxicating perfume. It reveals the impossible nearness of the sky. After taking laudanum, there are times when I know, if I just stretched up a bit more, I could brush my fingertips against the stars.

And yet there are other senses that laudanum seems to extinguish altogether. The sense of memory, for one. The sense of guilt, the sense of honour; it erases all of these rather well.

I am glad, for to be without memory, guilt, or honour is an advantage in my line of work. I take laudanum to fall asleep when sleep refuses to come, and also when being awake has become too… complicated.

Mostly I take it when a phantom voice rises stubbornly to the surface of my mind, claiming to be a messenger from the ruins of long ago. It calls that familiar name:

Jessamine!

Jessamine!

It even uses that word, the one that is no longer mine to speak, or think: love –

This is all very interesting, lovely. But really, what is the point of dwelling on the past? It is the future that counts. Our future.

His name is Weed! I remember now. Oh, how I loved him! You promised to bring me to him, Oleander. Will you keep your promise?

Of course, lovely. Very soon, I will. Although I cannot guarantee what kind of reception you will get. As I recall, he could be somewhat priggish, and you are quite a bit changed from the simple country girl he once knew.

I suppose I am… I had not thought of that.

He may even be repelled by you. You are a murderer, after all. Your wits are addled by opium, and you can hardly claim to have been faithful. You have the sweaty horse trader to thank for that.

He will revile me for a monster – do not take me to him, Oleander, I beg you! I would not have him see what I have become –

Silly girl. Of course I will take you to him. It is always pleasant to pay a call on an old friend, and a promise is a promise. But first we have work to do. I wish you to meet some acquaintances of mine. They are men of ambition and vision, who can appreciate your true worth… not like that sanctimonious what's-his-name…

He is right, I know.

Oleander is always right. I see that now.

Strange that I did not see it before.

13

1st November

Every day I learn fresh wonders from this wise
garden of Padua, and from my brave and generous
teacher, the signora.

I dare not record it all here lest this book fall
into the wrong hands. But there are some things I
cannot keep locked in my heart. Just as the Orto
botanico serves as a better angel to the poison
garden at Hulne Abbey, perhaps my own diary will
in some way make up for Thomas Luxton's diary of

*wickedness, now safely locked away. I hope it will,
at least.*

*The autumn weather in Padua is fair – cool,
sunny days mixed with days of soft rain – but
the people are uneasy. There is talk of revolution
everywhere I go.*

*Not a day goes by but I think of the preacher at
the crossroads. "The end is near," he bleated as he
died at my hands.*

*It is too late to trade my life for his, and for that
I will always mourn. But I would surely give my life
to prove the preacher wrong.*

SIGNORA BAGLIONI BEGINS EVERY lesson the
same way: "What does Oleander want?"

"Power."

"How does he gain power?"

"Through Jessamine."

"And what is his weapon?"

"Poison."

"Correct. He will use poison, somehow, to draw

Jessamine into his web of evil. Therefore you must learn to combat poison. You will master as many cures as you can. The knowledge the plants give you is priceless, Weed, but you cannot rely on them to save you." She piles the table high with books, with diagrams, with measuring spoons and vials of dried leaves and ground root powders.

I do as she instructs, but it hardly seems enough, for who knows when or where Oleander will choose to strike? Signora Baglioni says it does not matter: We must do something, and the longer Oleander waits to reveal himself, the more time we have to arm ourselves with the skills to defeat him.

So I study, and learn: about poisons, remedies, and the old lore from the collection that the signora thinks might help us understand Oleander's strength and weakness. We find many tales of the underworld and demons that live in realms below the earth. One story among them haunts my dreams: the one in which Hades, king of the dead, steals a human girl to be his bride. Her name is Persephone, and all of nature mourns her loss, for her mother is goddess of the harvest. As long as Hades keeps her in the underworld, the crops stop growing. The spring will not come.

Is this is how the earth grieves? It will be nothing compared to my grief, if some harm comes to Jessamine.

When my lessons are done, it is my turn to teach, as the signora and I agreed. I tell her all I know of the plants: the way they think about death, the flowers' vanity about their beauty, and the healing plants' pride in their powers. I tell her how the potted herbs on her windowsill chatter excitedly when she enters the room. I even tell her the way the trees sometimes speak in pompous riddles, and the ancient stories they like to tell. She writes it all down with a shaking hand.

"Such treasures to add to the collection!" She replaces the stopper in the ink and gently blots the paper. "How I wish my father and grandfather were alive to hear these."

"Why does your hand tremble so?"

She looks away and flexes her fingers. "It is one thing to spend one's life believing that plants have souls. It is quite another to have someone sit and dictate the words of the trees to you. You have seen the world in full your whole life long, but for the rest of us…"

Her voice trails off, but later I see her standing motionless by her potted herbs. Listening, perhaps. And then shaking her head in wonder.

I stay in her small spare room and earn my keep by working in the garden. I have become adept at throwing out the drunken medical students at daybreak. And I think – I hope – I have begun to earn the trust of the plants of the *Orto botanico*.

Daily, on my knees, I beg for news of Jessamine's whereabouts. The meadowsweet praises my courage, the creeping rosemary weeps for my loneliness, the yarrow urges me to obey Signora Baglioni – but they will not tell me where to find Jessamine.

"She has been touched by evil, but I know her heart is pure," I say to them. "Can you give me any news? You will know her easily. She has the fresh beauty of a blushing pink rose. Her hair is the colour of sunshine on wheat."

Every day their answer is the same. *We cannot find the girl you seek.*

"Why? Is she dead?"

If she were dead, her form would have returned to the earth, and the plants would know of this. They curl their leaves in apology. *We cannot find the girl you seek.*

Even these noble plants talk in riddles. Why can they not find her? Is she sailing across some lifeless sea? Wandering the great polar icecaps? Even in the depths of the driest desert, mesquite trees and cactus grow. Surely there is some plant on this Earth that has caught a glimpse of her, somewhere.

It is as if Jessamine no longer exists.

The signora begins today's lesson by ordering me to put on my coat and go with her. I know better than to question her instructions. I leap to obey and together we begin walking at a brisk pace.

I note that she is not wearing her usual gardening trousers, but a long skirt and a pair of sturdy heeled shoes. "We are going to see a colleague of mine at the university," she explains. "Dr. Marco Carburi is his name. He is a famous chemist. I believe we need his help."

"But I have learned every remedy and antidote you have taught me."

"You have done very well. There are many poisons with known antidotes. The university library documents them all, and thanks to the *Orto botanico*, we have access to virtually every plant called for in their preparation. However – this way, please, keep up! – we do not know what poison Oleander will use. Or what combination of poisons." She stops. "Weed, have you ever heard of a substance called mithridatum?"

"No."

She resumes walking, even faster than before. "It is named after King Mithridates. He was the ruler of Pontus, on the Black Sea, almost two millennia ago. Every king fears assassination, but Mithridates feared poison above all, for it was believed his own mother had poisoned his father to secure power for herself. Every day of his life starting in childhood, he took small quantities of the most powerful poisons, so that gradually he would develop a tolerance for them."

The thought of wilfully ingesting poison nearly makes me gag.

"But that was not enough for the worried king," the signora continues as we cross the narrow cobblestone streets. "He also developed what he claimed was a universal antidote, a complex mixture of dozens of healing herbs that could nullify any poison. This antidote came to be called mithridatum."

"It would be a substance of great value," I say, thinking once more of Thomas Luxton.

"Indeed. After the king's death, the great Roman general Pompey stole the notebooks containing the instructions for making mithridatum, so that his own physicians might try to copy it. Many versions of the formula have come down through the centuries. Some of the 'improvements' are not what I would call scientific. The flesh of vipers. Powdered unicorn horn." She shakes her head in contempt. "I have learned that Dr. Carburi has been trying to re-create the true formula.

If he has succeeded, and can be persuaded to share what he knows, I believe that preparing a supply of mithridatum will be to our great advantage."

Her eyes light up. "Weed, if Dr. Carburi does have such a formula, perhaps you might ask the healing plants of the *Orto botanico* if it could be improved upon. Would they be able to determine that?"

"They might," I say, suddenly uneasy. I know Signora Baglioni's intentions are good. The *Orto botanico* seeks only to heal. Yet the task she proposes is the same one Thomas Luxton once gave me – to go to the garden and bring back the plants' knowledge for the use of humans.

Is the line between good and evil only this? Some slight difference in intention?

The plant that kills is the plant that cures; all that matters is the dose. I know this to be true. What of me, then? And Oleander? Are we, too, made of the same substance, somehow?

"Here we are," Signora Baglioni says, gazing up at the grand university building. "The *Palazzo Bo*."

I stop her before she can open the door. "Did King Mithridates's scheme work? Did taking small doses of poison really make him immune to its power?"

"It worked all too well," she says. "At the end of his life, defeated and besieged by his enemies, King Mithridates refused to be taken alive. He slaughtered his wives and children and then tried to kill himself. But his resistance to poison was so strong he could not die. In the end, he had to order one of his soldiers to slay him with a sword."

She lifts her hand to knock. "Ironic, isn't it? A man who spent his whole life avoiding poisonous plots dies at the simple thrust of a blade. A common pickpocket could have done as much. But death is death, I suppose, no matter how it comes." She raps three times, and we wait. "I must warn you: Dr. Carburi is a brilliant man, but prone to theatrics. We shall see what he has in store today."

We arrive at his classroom just as Dr. Carburi is on his way out. "Did you forget about our appointment?" Signora Baglioni says, sounding cross, as the doctor grabs his coat and bag.

"Not at all, signora," he says airily, locking the door behind him. "I intend for you and your young companion – Weed, is it? Curious name – to join me; we will talk on the way. But hurry, we only have a few minutes."

"Where are we going?" I ask as he leads us deeper into the university building.

"To the anatomy theatre," he answers with satisfaction, turning down yet another maze of hallways. "Professor Scarpa is dissecting today. Not to be missed!" Signora Baglioni looks impatient, but Dr. Carburi either fails to notice or purposely ignores her. "Is it your first time to the anatomy theatre?" he asks me. "How marvellous for you. I prefer to watch the proceedings from the topmost tier, but you ought to see the auditorium from this level as well. From the corpse's point of view, you might say."

He leads us inside. It is a theatre, to be sure, in the shape of an oval, with six tiers of seats stacked one upon the next. At the centre of the lowest level is an empty table.

As I gaze up and around, a trio of musicians enters from behind us. Dr. Carburi nods a greeting. To me he whispers, "Scarpa always insists that music be played during his dissections. He says it keeps his hand steady."

"There was a reason for our meeting today," Signora Baglioni interjects. "It is a matter of some importance."

"Mithridatum, yes," Dr. Carburi replies smoothly, as if he had been about to mention it himself. "I have developed three versions that seem promising. The difficulty, of course, is testing them, for I am not so unscrupulous as to poison a man simply to find out if I can cure him. Therefore I cannot guarantee they will work. It seems we are blocking the musicians. Signora Baglioni, Signor Weed, let us ascend." With a grand gesture, he herds us back to the stairs.

"Even untested, the formulas would still be of academic interest to us." Signora glances meaningfully at me. I can guess what her look means: she will expect me to ask the *Orto botanico* to reveal if any of the antidotes will work. "We have no wish to gain profit from your work – but as one scholar to another, would you be willing to share your discoveries?"

"You may have the formulas, of course." We follow Dr. Carburi up the wooden stairs with carved balustrades that lead from one tier of seats to the next. "But as curiosities only, not as a prescription! And speaking of cures: there is something else I meant to tell you, Signora. A bit of gossip that may interest you."

He pauses on the landing, and lowers his voice. "I have received word that a party of revellers, drawn from the highest ranks of English nobility, will be descending on Padua for Martinmas. They will be housed in the great villas along the Brenta Canal, between Venice and Padua. They will be travelling in secret."

"Why?"

"For privacy, perhaps. As part of their itinerary, they are coming to see me."

"Not your infamous treatments, Marco!"

Amusement plays over his features. He turns to me. "You seem like a young man of the world, Signor Weed. In England they call it the French pox. In France they call it the Neapolitan pox."

Signora Baglioni snorts. "Yes, and in Naples they call it the English plague. What Professor Carburi refers to is the disease doctors call syphilis."

"Ignore the signora's scorn, young man, for it is undeserved. The truth is, I am considered an expert in treating this terrible illness. My patients come from all over Europe, from the highest ranks of society. They seek me out for my discretion, as well as for the ingenuity of my methods."

"Your methods are painful and of little help."

"Correction, Signora: My methods are excruciating and completely ineffective. They are also highly profitable."

"It is disgraceful."

"But my patients insist! Really, they have no other options."

"They might try keeping away from whores."

214

He shrugs and turns to me. "The signora's remedy is quite impractical. We are speaking of wealthy, powerful men on holiday abroad. Take away their whores, and the enterprise loses all meaning."

He smiles charmingly at Signora Baglioni, but her scowl deepens. "Moneyed Englishmen debauching their way through the Veneto is nothing new," she says. "What does this gossip signify?"

"My sources tell me King George himself will be among the party."

The signora's eyes widen. "The King of England? But why would he travel to Italy when half of Europe is at war? It is madness."

"Agreed. Whoever has convinced the king to leave the safety of England is a traitor. I fear a trap is being laid even now."

He lays a hand on my shoulder. "I am sure the signora has told you, if you don't already know: This region has a long and gruesome history of political assassination by poison. In Venice there was an official committee, the Council of Ten, which met to vote on whom to poison next. The French would find it admirably democratic."

By now we have reached the uppermost tier. Dr. Carburi pauses to catch his breath. "That they bring the English king here bodes very ill indeed, and all but guarantees that we will be blamed for whatever happens to him. It will bring war to our city. A royal assassination would be the end of Padua, the university, everything."

"But why would someone kill the King?" I ask, ashamed of my ignorance.

"Revolution." Dr. Carburi wipes his brow with a crimson silk square. "Murder the King and chaos reigns, just long enough for a fresh crop of tyrants to seize power. Come inside now; we have climbed as high as we can, and it is almost time – "

He steps through a small door into the auditorium.

We follow. The view from this uppermost tier is dizzying, like looking down a well. The coffin-shaped table waits below.

"What a view, eh?" He turns once more to the

216

signora. "The *Orto botanico* – are there not plants within it that could be used to cause harm?"

"Of course there are, for one who has the knowledge and skill."

He nods. "Be careful who enters. Be wary of theft. It is a pity the plants themselves cannot stand guard. The things they must witness! If only they could speak…"

From the seats below us comes a ripple of excited chatter, as two men in blood-stained smocks enter. Together they lean on one side of the dissecting table, until it rotates all the way around. A woman's naked corpse lies strapped to the other side. The crowd gasps and applauds.

"Bravo!" Dr. Carburi throws off his cape, revealing a slightly crushed orchid boutonniere pinned to his lapel. He removes a small telescope from his pocket. "That double-sided table is a marvellous touch."

Beware, the dying orchid whispers.

As the two assistants lock the table in place, a tall man in a flowing white coat strides into the theatre

217

and takes a low bow. When he straightens, he lifts his right arm. He holds a gleaming silver knife in his hand.

"Professor Scarpa," Carburi says eagerly, extending his opera glass and holding it to one eye. "The dissection is about to begin."

"Why?" I whisper under my breath. Signora Baglioni gives me a startled look, but says nothing. Carburi is too busy focusing his opera glass to notice.

The violinist raises his instrument, and the other players follow suit. As the knife makes the first cut, the musicians begin to play.

I lean forward, as if to see better, but in truth I seek to get closer to the fading bloom. With its last morsel of strength, the orchid says: *When the Prince of Poisons wants the world to know his might, what better way than to poison a king?*

BE CHARMING, LOVELY. That was Oleander's final instruction. *These men do my bidding, though they do not know it. They think the voice of providence speaks to them, or the voice of their own ambition, but they obey me nevertheless. I want you to serve them freely, for their purpose and mine are aligned – for now.*

I direct the coach driver to let me off at the servants' entrance of a nobleman's estate. A silent butler with thinly-arched eyebrows bids me come inside and leads me to a private chamber, richly appointed. I still have not been told the purpose of this summons.

I count six men, seated in chairs around the fire or standing, leaning against the back of a divan or examining a book from the library shelves. The three youngest are no more than thirty and seem virile and eager, with flaring nostrils like racehorses. The older men are full-bellied and bandy-legged, foolish in their white wigs, ruffled lace shirtfronts, and velvet waistcoats.

They eye me with grave curiosity, and some scepticism.

"This?" a younger one says to the eldest man. "This pale wraith is the skilled one you spoke of?"

"She is. Come in, my dear. Someone get our guest a glass of whiskey."

"Perhaps later," I say quickly. I have already taken an extra dose of laudanum to steady my nerves. I am at my best now, fearless and without shame, but anything more will make me reckless.

"As you wish. We have been told you are a young lady of the utmost discretion, is that so?"

"Yes." I look around. All eyes are upon me.

"In that case, welcome. We are the founders and members of a private club. Our membership is select, our existence secret. Do you know what a scorpion is?"

His patronising tone makes me bristle. "I prefer to work with plants, not insects," I retort. "But yes, I do know that scorpions poison their prey. Most are not venomous enough to be lethal to larger animals; only a few are dangerous to humans." I meet his challenging gaze. "And, given the right boot, all can easily be crushed underfoot."

He laughs. "Well said! You live up to your reputation quite well. You have arrived just in time, Miss Belladonna. We of the Scorpion Society always begin our meetings with a prayer. Gentlemen, please join me in speaking the assassin's creed."

The men bow their heads and recite.

*"The Old One asks: Is it better to be the assassin,
        or the king?
Surely, my lord, it is better to be the assassin.*

*For the names of murdered kings are soon
    forgotten.
But no one forgets the glint of the blade.
The strangling cord.
The poisoned chalice.
These are the weapons the people fear.
These are the weapons that haunt their sleep."*

"And whatever weapon the people fear gives power to those who wield it. May that power be ours; to use it as we see fit," the man finishes, to which his fellow conspirators reply, "Amen."

These are the Hashshashin, I think. *And I am one of them now.*

They gather chairs in a circle and invite me to sit with them. Then the plotting begins. They call one another by secret names, each taken from a different killing plant: Foxglove. Chrysanthemum. Rhododendron. Narcissus. I listen as they spin their web of schemes, each treasonous thought a fresh log on the bonfire of wickedness they build together – it seems they will not stop until the blaze consumes all of England. Each speaks in turn, but their purpose has a single voice.

"Revolution is a healing plague that leaps across borders and spreads from one nation to the next. Our country already has the blessed infection. Many in England long for change, and we count ourselves among the most powerful of these. As such, we wish to bring the sickness to a head, so to speak, so that the purge may run its full course."

"As a doctor lets blood to release bad humours, we too must bleed this patient, this England, until the dross has been emptied from its veins."

"There will be blood, make no mistake. Blood in plenty. But first, there is a tumour to be excised. A tumour in the shape of a crown…"

Their plan reaches beyond England's borders, for it will be safer that way, abroad and out of reach of the royal guard. There is mention of a ball, fancy dress, a masquerade… a sealed bottle of wine, uncorked in front of the King to allay suspicion… a deadly glass to be prepared at the last moment, tainted and served by a deceptively attractive messenger, ruthless and beautiful, lacking all fear....

The grey-haired man whom the others call Monkshood abruptly pulls me onto his lap. With one liver-spotted hand he holds me fast; the other strokes my thigh, as if I were a pet Pomeranian dog. I writhe from his grasp. When he does not let me go, I slap him hard across the face.

The crack of the blow silences the room. Free of his grip and on my feet, I am quickly seized by two of the men.

The grey-haired man wipes a trickle of blood from the corner of his mouth, and smiles. "Ruthless indeed. And beautiful," he says, as if I am not in the room. "A dish fit for a king."

The others chuckle. I struggle to free myself but cannot. The one called Narcissus takes my chin in his hand and jerks my face to the light. He looks at my eyes with a clinical interest, first one, then the other.

"In addition to your other virtues, you, my dear, are an opium eater of the first rank," he concludes.

"How charmingly decadent. I hope it will not interfere with the efficient *execution* of your duties."

The men nod approvingly at his choice of words.

"It gives me courage," I retort. "It frees me to do my work."

"Does it? Give her some more, then," one of the men instructs, laughing. "Perhaps it will make her a bit friendlier."

They fetch me a drink, whiskey and laudanum mixed, and then another, and soon I am laughing too, my head thrown back, as I toss my raven-black hair and dance before the fire for my appreciative fellow assassins.

No broken, lost soul am I among these powerful men. No; I am triumphant; I am all that they wish me to be, and more. The poison in my veins thrums with the joy of a homecoming.

And all the while, Oleander's words bear me aloft like warm, caressing wings.

Dance, my beautiful, deadly beloved. Forget about these panting fools, and dance with abandon, for me alone… for soon you will be mine… but first, you shall be the king's…

# 15

3rd November

Later I told Signora Baglioni about the warning I received. We both agree; the orchid's meaning was clear. Oleander himself is behind this plot to kill the king.

Why? To demonstrate his power, no doubt. To loose fear and chaos on the world, for that is his pleasure. Yet it is Jessamine who holds the key to his strength. And what could Jessamine have to do with such an evil deed as this one?

The discovery has made our work all the more

urgent, for Martinmas is scarcely more than a week away.

For two days and two nights, Signora has devoted herself to creating the different formulas for mithridatum that Dr. Carburi gave her. Untested, they are of no use to us, but when I remind her of this, she waves me away and keeps working, all the while muttering and cursing aloud in her native tongue.

Again and again she has sent me to the garden to gather the required leaves and herbs. This morning she finally completed three vials of the legendary antidote – one of each formula.

"One of them will save the life of your king, but which? Take them all," she said, exhausted, for she has scarcely slept. "Bring them to the garden. See if the plants can advise us."

In truth, I care little for the fate of this king, or any other. The fields and forests do not follow the boundaries of nations. But if Oleander would use this royal murder for his own ends, I will do what I must to stop him.

And if the poison prince is close, I fear – and

hope – that Jessamine cannot be far away.
I will be ready.

THE TREE SIGNORA CALLS the Palm of St. Peter is
the oldest plant in the garden, and the wisest. It is not
happy to see me, but there is no plant I would trust
more to test these precious vials.

"Again?" the palm says crossly when I kneel before
it. "Already we have watched as you helped yourself
to ginger, saffron, cardamom, shepherd's purse, anise,
St. John's wort, cassia bark, and hartwort root, and
at least two dozen others. Is there a plant left in this
garden that has not been pruned to the ground?" Its
fan-shaped clusters of leaves quiver with irritation.
"Or have you come to harvest me this time?"

"Forgive me," I say, my head bowed. The palm
tree is not as big as the ancient oaks and pines of the
Northumberland forests, but it is more than twice
my height, and the authority it commands is great. "I
know I have taken much from the garden. I come at
the bidding of the signora. She is trying to create a

remedy for poison. It is very important that she succeeds."

"To you, perhaps. If foolish humans wish to poison one another, how does it matter to us?"

"It matters a great deal," I say hotly. "For it is Oleander himself who is making his power known – "

"*Silence!*" The rough hairs on the palm's grey trunk bristle in anger. "Do you think you know better than we what danger is posed by the upstart prince? He is not the concern of *you humans*."

"He is surely my concern, for he is my enemy," I snap back in anger. "He is a danger to Jessamine, my beloved – the girl I have asked you about so many times, the one you cannot seem to find, anywhere…"

I catch myself – I ought not to rage at this wise being, when I have come to beg a favour. Still, the palm's tone softens. "Seasons change, Weed. Winter comes, and you cannot stand in the way of it. One must accept that." Its leaves curl and uncurl again, in a gentle reproof. "Now. Why are you here?"

I take out the three vials. "These are the three mixtures of antidote the signora has prepared. We need to know if any of them has the power to stop poison."

"Place a drop upon my broadest leaf. One drop of each, please."

I obey. The palm quivers and mutters. "Yes. There is power here. One greater, two lesser."

"Is the greater power enough to combat strong poisons in the body of a human?"

"It is great," the palm concludes. "But I do not know how great a poison it will meet with. I do not know the strength of the human in question. I am old and wise, Weed, but I cannot know the unknowable. I cannot say whether it is enough for your purposes. Only that it is powerful."

I know the signora will be disappointed with this answer, but the palm speaks the truth. "And which was the more powerful mixture? The first drop, the second, or the third?"

"One greater, two lesser," the palm repeats.

My anger flares once more. "Surely one such as you cannot be afraid of the evil prince. Why will you not tell me?"

"You are the one who seeks this knowledge, Human Who Hears. You are the one who must pay the price of knowing." After a time, the palm adds, "The Prince is evil, yes – but he is one of us. We cannot take sides with a human against him."

I rise. "I understand. Thank you for your aid." I cannot help myself from asking one last time: "Has there been any news of Jessamine?"

The palm sways thoughtfully in the breeze. "There is a girl," it says, and chants:

"Her hair as black as raven wings.

Her lips red as a poppy flower.

Her heart as merciless as the belladonna berry.

Her will as deadly."

"That cannot be her," I say, my heart breaking.

"In that case – we cannot find the girl you seek," the palm says, and falls silent.

231

Luckily the signora has stepped into the courtyard to tend to her grapes. It takes me but a moment to prepare the vilest mixture I can think of. Hemlock, hellebore, wormwood, arsenic, wolfsbane, plus a half dozen others. All equally deadly.

I could add honey to mask the taste, but there is no need. I will not give myself even a moment to reconsider; I lift the glass and drink. My body cries out against it, my throat gags as if a noose were tightening around my neck, but my will is stronger.

I drain the last drop of noxious potion, and look up. Signora Baglioni stands in the doorway, caught in midstride. Her eyes move to the empty glass in my hand.

"Signora Baglioni, I am sorry to impose upon you," I say. I must speak quickly, while I can. "Very shortly I will fall ill. When I do, please administer your first formula for mithridatum."

She takes a step toward me. "Weed – what have you done?"

"If I do not recover within the hour, give me the

second formula. If that does not work, the third." I pause. Something is wrong with my eyes. The room blurs, and my hand goes to my forehead. "If it comes to the third, it is probably best not to wait too long. I shall have to trust your judgment... about that..."

"Reckless fool!" she cries, seizing the glass from me and sniffing it. "What did you drink?"

I find myself leaning against the wall of her kitchen. Either I am slipping down, or the floor is rising up to meet me. My belly feels suddenly full of broken glass. "One of the three antidotes is likely to work. The Palm of St. Peter told me so. We only need to discover which one – "

"*Likely* to work! You *idiot*! You should not have risked yourself in this way. You are much too valuable – without you there is no hope – "

Those are the last words I hear.

The King of England is not as brutish as he might be, given that his most casual request carries the force of law. I should be grateful for that, I suppose.

233

Most days I am the one chosen to serve him his food. Afterwards I dance for him or sing to him. When he is ill, I fetch a chamber pot for him to vomit into. I bathe his face with a cool, wet cloth as if he were a sick child and tell him our difficult journey will be over in another day or two, no more.

I am one royal handmaiden of many, but my orders were to make sure I became his favourite. This I have done. It was not difficult; he may be a king, but he is also a man. My lavish attentions made him welcome my company, and a few drops of a carefully prepared aphrodisiac guaranteed that he would prefer me above all others.

When he asks me to stay behind after the meal is done, I obey. When we are alone, I pretend just enough impudence to rouse his passion. When he wishes to quench a rebellion, I resist. But he is victorious, always, for he is the king, beloved of his people, God's anointed ruler and on Earth supreme head of the Church of England.

And two days hence, I will kill him in cold blood.

Not here, in his private stateroom aboard ship, where it would be all too easy to do. No – I am ordered to do it in public, in front of the English court and before the eyes of Europe, so that my master's will might strike fear into the hearts of the most powerful men in the world.

At last I can tally the true price of my bargain with Oleander. If I succeed in my task, I will be killed on the instant. If I fail, my fate is the same. My new acquaintances in the Scorpion Society made that very clear.

Either way, this is how my final days on Earth will be spent: on this rolling, stomach-churning journey in the belly of a ship, the traitorous bedmate of a seasick king. I would laugh, or weep, or leap overboard, if not for the laudanum.

And if not for Oleander. Am I mad to say it? I know he is my downfall, my destroyer, yet he is the only companion I have left. His incorporeal presence has become my north star. His constant devotion is all that has kept me from hurling myself into the sea.

235

He guides me and comforts me. He tells me what special herbs to add to the laudanum, to keep me indifferent and as pleasure-seeking as a cat. He whispers words of adoration to me all night long, until I can scarcely sleep from longing.

I wish I could touch you, I tell him.

Would that I could possess you as the fat king does. But soon, lovely. Soon.

My every waking moment, he praises my beauty, even as I lift my gown and offer myself to my sovereign, His Majesty King George III, by the grace of God, King of Great Britain and Ireland, Defender of the Faith. Whose life and reign it is my destiny to end.

❦

The slap of wetness against a thin hull. The steady splash of a gondolier's oar moving through the water. These are the sounds I wake to.

Signora – I try to speak, but no words come. With difficulty I open my eyes.

Someone has dressed me in a gentleman's Sunday

clothes – a crisp linen shirt, a matching frock coat and breeches. The clothes are not my own and are over-large for my frame. My feet are bare.

I am propped up against the side of a gondola, wearing a broad-brimmed straw hat against the sun. My right hand trails over the side. The still water of the canal is cold, slimy, unpleasant. I wish to lift my hand from the water but cannot.

I cannot seem to move at all.

Around me, the students are laughing, joking. Full of high spirits, bragging about their pranks. Somehow I know their names. Moonseed. Larkspur. Dumbcane. Snakeweed.

"You are not medical students," I say, or try to. "Look. There is dirt still clinging to your roots."

They laugh. "You are covered in earth too, Master Weed. But perhaps that is because we have just dug you up from your grave."

"My grave?"

"Of course! Where else do you think the bodies come from?"

237

The gondola passes beneath a footbridge and moves into shadow. All is darkness.

It will be darkness without end, this time, I think with relief. Finally I have reached the end of this terrible agony I am already too near death to feel... darkness is nearly here, and with it, peace...

And then there is light. And pain.

Like the world itself, I spin. Night turns into day, day into night, again and again.

When the spinning stops, I am flat on my back, spread-eagled. My clothes are gone.

A *click*, as the dissection table is locked into place.

I dare to open my eyes. Faces, hundreds of them, near and impossibly high, all staring at me. Hungry with anticipation.

I struggle to rise but am held down with straps.

Oleander appears before me, silver-haired, his dark wings folded against his back. One arm is raised, and something sharp gleams in his hand. He gazes down with mocking emerald eyes, the same vivid green as my own.

"Weed! What a surprise. We were all quite sure you were dead."

"Not – not yet – " I gasp. The pain is returning, spreading quickly, too quickly –

"So I see. But it won't be long now. And the crowds have already gathered. The preparations have been made. It is much too late to change our plans. What is it your mountebank used to say? The show must go on? Music, please," he commands some unseen players.

But I hear no music – just the hoarse cry of the raven –

KRAAAAAAAAAAAAAAHHH!

as the blade of ice comes plunging down…

Oleander?

Yes, lovely?

I have been wondering: Is there a worse crime than to kill God's anointed King?

It is dreadfully wicked, to be sure. But there are so many different sorts of crimes, and each one is worse than the last. One can scarcely keep track of them all.

Do you think it is worse than killing one's own father?

Not many people get to experience both, lovely. Count yourself fortunate in that respect. But why ask such pointless questions? I hope you are not having second thoughts. For I would be so very disappointed if you were to break your word.

No. I know it does not matter. I am going to hell, no matter what. I was just curious. May I ask you something else?

Curiosity killed the cat, my dear.

Still, I wish to know. Is Weed alive?

Weed! Why do you ask?

I – I am not sure. I would like to say goodbye to him, I suppose.

Too late, lovely. I had been meaning to tell you. Weed has taken poison.

No! I don't believe you.

I assure you, he has taken enough poison to kill ten men. Rather excessive, in my opinion. I am sorry if the news upsets you. But you know I would not lie to you about a subject so near to my heart.

I weep.

Quiet, lovely. Dry your tears. You will wake His Majesty.

I cannot stop.

Have another dose of laudanum. It will calm you.

More? But I am already so dizzy – my mind is in a fog –

The more you take, the closer I can come. If you took just a little more, I am quite sure we would be able to feel each other's touch. Wouldn't that be a comfort to you, in this time of grief? Good girl – there, my wings enfold you even now. Can you feel me?

I think I can. Oleander – I will be dead when all this is over, won't I?

Such questions. You must trust me, lovely. When your work is done, you will be with me. I am your eternal reward.

Promise me.

You will find your refuge at last. I promise.

"Fool, fool fool! Staking your life on the word of a two-hundred-year-old palm tree. Weed? Can you hear me?"

I grunt. Two agile fingers pry my right eye open. Through the slit I see the face of Signora Baglioni. Worried, angry. More angry, I think. She lets go, and darkness falls again. I try to move but can only manage a groan.

"Still alive. *Bene!* For I would hate to lose the chance to scold you for what you have done. The moment you can stand up, I intend to give you a tongue-lashing that will be far worse than any poison."

Now I open my eyes myself, just a little. The light is blinding. Another groan escapes my lips.

"How do you feel?"

"You seem convinced I am alive. I am not so sure." I turn my head from side to side. My brain rolls like a cannonball in my skull. "Was it the third formula?"

"It was. Lucky you. You almost died. I gave you the third mixture as soon as I could get it down your throat, but even then I thought it was too late."

"How long have I been ill?"

"Three days. The King and his party arrived in Padua yesterday. You have come back from the dead just in time."

I struggle to sit up and manage to get my feet on the floor. The room whirls once, but settles. The signora hands me a glass of lemon water. "Drink," she orders. "Tomorrow evening you will attend a royal masquerade ball, here in Padua. King George III and his followers will revel until the small hours of the morning. You will make sure that nothing sinister ends up in the King's wine. If he falls suddenly ill for any reason, you will administer the mithridatum – whose effectiveness you can now vouch for personally."

I hand the empty glass back to the signora and stretch my limbs. I am hungry, of all things. A good sign. "How did you manage to obtain an invitation to such an exclusive event?"

She laughs. "I have many friends in Padua, you know! And who said you would be going as a guest? You are the entertainment, Weed. You will make roses bloom for the King."

16

11th November. The Feast of St Martin.

*My costume for the masquerade ball can only be
called miraculous. Signora Baglioni has obtained a
black silk suit with an emerald-green waistcoat and
a black velvet mask to cover my face. The plants
of the Orto botanico have contributed their most
delicate tendrils and most fragrant blooms. From
these the signora has fashioned a living cape of
greenery and flowers.*

With the help of these brave plants, tonight I

will give my greatest performance. If only Jessamine
could be there to see it.

"Bellissimo," Signora Baglioni murmurs,
making the final adjustments to my cape. "I wish I
could see the faces of those traitorous English aristocrats when you walk in the door."

"You are not coming?"

She puts down her shears. "I must stay and watch
over the *Orto botanico*. Evil will be afoot in Padua
tonight. We must both be careful."

"Do not be afraid, signora. I will make sure no
harm comes to the king."

"I hope so." She frowns. "I confess, Weed. I am
troubled. I fear it is no accident that the Prince of
Poisons has come here to demonstrate his power.
Here, to Padua. Why?"

"I thought the English court planned to see Dr.
Carburi, for his profitable treatments?" I say it to make
her smile, but she will not.

"That is the reason they gave." She sounds

unconvinced. "You once told me of your first meeting with Oleander. You were a child, a stowaway on board a ship. Remember?"

"All too well. We were attacked by pirates. Some of the crew were slain. The rest, captured and bound." If I close my eyes, I can smell the salt spray and hear the cries of the dying men, so I make sure to keep my gaze fixed on the signora. "I killed the pirates myself, with poison that Oleander instructed me to put in their food."

"Did you ever wonder why he saved your life?"

Her question makes me uneasy. "If Oleander had his way, we would all be murderers. It must have amused him to turn a frightened child into a killer of men."

"True. But you were no ordinary child. Perhaps he had a reason for saving you. Perhaps he imagines some dark purpose for your talents." She hands me my mask. "Perhaps he brought his wicked scheme to Padua because he knew you were here, Weed."

"His purposes and mine are opposed." Anger

seizes me. "My dearest wish is to destroy him."

"Yet if not for Oleander, you would not have lived to make that wish." She holds out a vial, filled with thick dark liquid, stoppered with a cork. It is the mithridatum. I stow it carefully in the pocket of my waistcoat, as the signora watches with a worried look.

"*Buona fortuna*, Weed." She stops me at the door. "Remember, the English King is not the only one in danger tonight. Oleander will bait his trap for you. You will have to be strong. You will have to be ready to choose – perhaps, to sacrifice – "

She does not need to say more.

I remember the terrible lessons taught by the poison garden at Hulne Abbey, when my beloved lay dying. The way I was forced to do that which repulsed me. How I was made to learn that my ideas of right and wrong would crumple like dead leaves under the weight of my love for Jessamine.

If I were given a choice between saving Jessamine and saving the King – which would I choose?

There is no time to wonder. I must go. Yet the

signora still clings to my arm.

"I was thinking, too, of that soldier who slew King Mithridates," she says in a low voice. "It is no small crime to murder a king, even if done out of loyalty. No doubt the man paid for his service with his life."

"He did what was asked of him." I say it to comfort her, but she shakes her head.

"As do we all. Still, it was very brave. I would have liked to have known that man." She kisses me good-bye, once on each cheek, and quickly turns away, but not before I see the tears in her eyes.

I understand: She does not expect to see me alive again.

The King's party travels to the *Palazzo della Ragione* in a slow procession through the streets of Padua. We are a spectacle, to be sure, a parade of English aristocrats and their whores, all in masks and costumes. The children point and stare, and dash into shadows when we get close.

No one knows who we are, or that the King of

England travels with us. If asked, we have been told to say we are wealthy English citizens on the Grand Tour, but I doubt there are many tourists who have travelled in such remarkable style.

"*Belladonna*," they call when they see me. Beautiful lady, indeed. I wear a Grecian sheath of black tulle, a mask adorned with purple orchids, and a spray of white oleander blossoms in my raven-black hair. The flowers are poisonous in themselves, but there is one special bloom that has been steeped in the killing dose I prepared myself, this very day.

My arms and neck are bare, and the sheer gown scarcely conceals my body, but I am past all modesty by now. As Oleander instructed, I have anointed my skin with the aphrodisiac mixture that helps keep the King in thrall to me. It will guarantee that no man stands in my way today, for my lightest touch will command any who comes near. Nor do I mind the November chill, for my blood runs quick and hot in my veins.

Prepare your morning tea as I bid you, Oleander urged when I awoke. *The nectar of the Hashshashin will give you all the courage you need.* I obeyed, and now there is not a drop of fear in me. My reactions seem unnaturally quickened, or else the rest of the world slowed. I feel as if I could pluck a raindrop out of the air as it fell.

I do not know who suggested a botanical theme for the masquerade – I heard it said it was because the *palazzo* sits above the fruit and vegetable markets of Padua – but the fancy suits my purposes well. The King himself is dressed as a sunflower, with a ruffled collar of bright orange framing his face. All the other masked revellers are bedecked with woven leaves and lavish arrangements of flowers.

"There," someone says as we turn. "The Palace of Reason." From the outside, the roof looks like the overturned hull of an enormous ship. In my mind I see people drowning, adrift in a storm-tossed sea. I hear their screams, the pleas for help, the choking cries –

Forgive me for not saving you, I think, *but I too am drowning, and will soon be dead.*

Then I blink, and the image disappears.

250

I climb the stairs with the other ladies of the court. Together we enter the *Salone*, the vast upstairs hall where the ball will take place.

I have never been in a room so large; its sheer size makes me dizzy. In keeping with our theme, the room has been filled with potted trees and garlands of blooming flowers. It is an unmoored Eden, an island of paradise floating in the heavens. All who enter gape at the stars painted on the vaulted ceiling and the frescoes along the walls that depict the twelve signs of the zodiac.

I, too, pause at each to admire them, until I get to the sign of the scorpion.

"*Couragio*, lovely. I will not let you fail."

I gasp. Oleander's voice is as familiar to me as my own thoughts, yet these words are not spoken within my mind, but from behind me. I turn. Standing before me is the Prince himself. His silver hair gleams in the torchlight, but the emerald shade of his eyes tugs at my heart – *no, do not think of Weed*, I tell myself, *it is much too late for that* –

"My powers increase by the day. I have you to thank for that, lovely. You have performed beyond my wildest expectations." His wings of leathery leaves make him seem just another extravagantly costumed guest – yet I cannot tell if he is real or an apparition. "I cannot stay long, but I would not have missed this night for the world. You look stricken, my dear – are you that surprised to see me?"

I can scarcely breathe. "Yes."

Good, he whispers, shimmering into thin air. *For I do so love surprises. As you will soon see.*

Signora Baglioni was wise to arrange things this way. The room is filled with plants, my allies. The platform stage lets me see all who are here.

I can spot the traitors easily. They are dressed as poisonous plants – foxglove, rhododendron, narcissus, monkshood – and when they pass near the potted trees that line the entrance to the *Salone*, the leaves tremble in alarm.

There has been much drink and dancing. Now

chairs have been arranged to face the stage. The sunflower king takes a seat near the back. Already he staggers from too much champagne. A ripe beauty hangs on each arm.

"Begin your amazing feats, Signor *Erbaccia*," he calls loudly. "For my dinner awaits, and my drink as well. And then – my bed!"

"As Your Majesty wishes," I say with a bow. Swirling my magnificent cape, I perform one miracle after another. I make tendrils of vine lengthen and curl into shapes in the air. Bundles of baby's breath and lavender bloom on my command.

The crowd shouts and claps for each feat in turn. They believe it to be some kind of trick, but a good one. Little do they know the true marvels that happen in front of their eyes.

As I used to do with the mountebank, I end with a rose. I produce a dozen unopened buds on fresh-cut stems. First I show them to an audience member near the front of my platform stage, a bald-pated man wreathed in boughs of pine.

Through his monocle, he examines each bud. "They are real, quite real," he announces to the crowd.

I place the roses in a vase. I bow low before them and make my request. Slowly, one by one, the roses bloom.

The applause is long and loud. I lift the full-blown roses and cradle them in my arms. Out of habit – or is it hope? – I scan the crowd, searching for the girl who most looks like Jessamine.

As has happened countless times before, my eyes light upon one pretty golden-haired face after another, and then move on in disappointment.

Until I see –

Jessamine. Ice-blue eyes staring from within a bruise-coloured mask.

Her hair is as dark as an undertaker's coat. Her soft, blushing cheeks are chiselled and pale as marble.

Her blood-red lips outline a mouth slack with shock.

I would not have recognised her without the mask. But it frames her eyes so I can see them apart from the rest of her. Jessamine's eyes. I would know them anywhere.

Those eyes are fixed on mine now. A stare of terror.

The King's fingers play idly on the bare skin of her neck. I have kissed the spot myself, right at the tender hollow of her throat.

Her crimson mouth forms the word – *Weed* –

Weed – dear God – it is Weed.

He nods and bows, and lets his gaze wander the room. For a moment his eyes seem to linger on mine. Yet he gives no sign; his expression does not change. Gallantly he hands a single rose to a squealing young woman near the stage and makes his exit.

I knew him at once; how could I not? The instant he took the stage I stood transfixed by every movement of his graceful form, those dark unruly curls, the flash of emerald in his eyes.

Only his manner is new. Once he was unused to human companionship and had an air of wariness about him. Now he has found his place in the world. His grace and quiet confidence would leave any woman breathless.

He cannot have recognised me – I pray he did not. Not only am I costumed and masked, but everything about me is altered, inside and out. To have Weed see me like this, ruby-lipped, in a dress of clinging gauze, steeped in a potion that keeps the King pawing at me like a drunken sailor, a deadly weapon pinned to my hair – it would be too much shame to bear.

Is there time to flee? Even now the bell rings for dinner. The guests take their places at the long banquet table and stand patiently beside their chairs, waiting for the King.

The King – my King, who I am about to murder. How can I perform this evil deed with Weed looking on? The sight of him awakens feelings in me I thought dead and buried. Love. Hope. The knowledge of right and wrong. They fight their way through the poisoned haze I have come to accept as my natural state.

Weed – I would cry his name aloud, not to the stars on the painted ceiling of this great hall, but to the real ones in the unseen heavens above. I would turn his name to a song of joy – but who would the singer be? Jessamine, or Belladonna? A monster bred to kill, like the Hashshashin? A soul damned for all eternity? Or a fallen, brutalised girl for whom there may yet be some slim hope of grace?

Members of the Scorpion Society stand like sentries at every door of the *Salone*. I know them by their costumes, for they are adorned with the flowers of their poisonous namesakes. Foxglove. Chrysanthemum. Rhododendron. Narcissus.

Any other men here I might be able to charm my way past, but not them. They know of my intoxicating tricks, and their eyes never leave me. If I try to escape, they will have me garroted in an instant.

There is no place to run. No place to hide.

The bell rings once more. I take a final desperate look around. I can no longer see Weed in the crowd.

If he did not recognise me, and left, it is the last

257

and greatest mercy I shall ever know. Now it is time to meet my fate.

Let the end come quickly, I beseech whatever god might listen to a killer's prayer. *For the King, and for me as well.*

Trailing his sunflower train, the King moves to the gilded chair at the head of the table. He sits, and the guests follow suit.

A priest leads a blessing, and fawning introductory remarks are made. A new man rises to speak. He is the one I know as Monkshood; it seems he is a high-ranking member of the court. He taps his glass and waits for silence.

"And now," he begins with false solemnity, "According to custom, we will mark the feast of St. Martin by uncorking a bottle of the season's new wine."

There are shouts of approval as a bottle is delivered to the table. Its label bears no words, but an image: a spray of oblong, leathery leaves topped with a cluster of white flowers – just like the ones pinned in my hair. A stone-faced servant prepares to pull the cork.

"Many say new wine is never as good as old," the traitor continues. "But that is not always true. Sometimes a change from the old is good. Change is natural, like the change of seasons. Not to be feared."

"You sound like a revolutionary, Charles!" someone calls. There is a ripple of uneasy laughter.

"And you sound like an aristocrat," he replies. "But we are not here to talk politics, surely. Tomorrow we fast; today we feast!"

"Hear, hear!"

"Uncork the new bottles and drain the old!"

As I take my place at the King's right hand, I make sure to brush close to the men who sit by him. The fog of desire I cast will erase all suspicion, for a short time, at least.

It will be long enough.

The King turns to me with heat in his eyes and offers his glass. "Fill this for me, girl. It will taste all the sweeter coming from your hands."

I let my fingers stroke the King's as I take the wine glass from him. "One last bloom for Your Majesty," I say. With a coy smile, I reach up to my hair and pluck the deadly blossom that waits there.

As I do, a rain of pure white petals falls from the garland of lilies overhead. They land at the feet of a young man dressed in black silk, with an emerald-green waistcoat the same colour as his eyes.

It is Weed. Dropping his cape of greenery, he has emerged from the shadows and now stands not ten paces away. His eyes are fixed, not on me, but on the wine glass in my hand.

Weed! How could I have forgotten the sweetness of life? Of goodness? Of love?

Too late, lovely.

The deadly oleander blossom is cradled in my palm.

It is much too late to change your mind.

The King watches me with eager eyes.

Smiling, I drop the blossom in the wine. I swirl the glass.

And then I drink.

# 17

I AM DYING, DROWNING *at the bottom of the Tyne once more. A searing pain splits my chest; my lungs are ready to burst. With my last atom of strength I kick and struggle to rise through the murk, away from the darkness, to the light, but it is so very far away —*

I gasp, and open my eyes. I am lying in Weed's arms.

"I know I am dead, but this cannot be hell," I whisper. "Where am I?"

His face floods with tenderness. "You are alive. You are safe. You are with me now."

I close my eyes again and sink into his warmth. His familiar earth scent. It is almost enough to make me forget everything that has happened – how long has it been since we held each other like this?

I do so love surprises…

The fantasy of bliss lasts but a moment, before I remember who and what I really am. How all is not as it was, and can never be again. My eyes fly open again, and I struggle to sit up.

"Where are we? There are men who would kill me if they found me." I look around. I am in a small, sun-drenched bedroom in what seems to be a private house. Every windowsill is lined with potted plants.

"We are safe, under the protection of a trusted friend. The men you speak of believe you are dead and will not pursue." His voice hardens. "I cannot say the same of their master."

"He is my master as well – Weed. I have fallen – "

He puts his arms around me and holds me as I weep. Finally he speaks. "I went to the masquerade to stop the King's murder. When I saw you there, so changed" – at this I sob – "I knew you were under the Prince's power. But until the lilies warned me about the deadly flower in your hair, I did not imagine the assassin would be you."

"You must think I am a monster."

He takes me by both arms. "I said those same words to you, once. Do you remember? I was sure you would hate me when you knew my true nature. Jessamine, you drank the poison meant for the King. Whatever wickedness has taken root in you, remember – in that moment you refused to do evil. At the cost of your own life, you refused."

"I was filled with shame, not goodness. My only wish was that you not have to witness the wretch I have become." I search his eyes. "I know what poison I put in that wine. Why am I not dead?"

He smiles. "After you fell to the ground, one of the men leaped up and cried, 'The King's glass was poisoned! The girl saved his life!' All was chaos. Swords were drawn, accusations of treachery were made. In the frenzy I caught you in my arms and tried to flee.

The traitors tried to stop me. With the help of friends, we escaped."

"The plants?"

He nods. "They tangled the men in vines, pinned them between branches, and held them back with thorns. Once outside, I gave you a powerful antidote. I had brought it with me to save the King's life. Instead, it saved yours."

"The King – what happened to him?"

"He is unharmed but furious. Now he and his guards know there are traitors in their midst. In the future they will not be so careless." He gaze softens. "My beloved, my Jessamine! To look in your eyes again is like being given a new life. They are beautiful. Innocent. Worthy of love. I would know them anywhere."

He kisses me then, tenderly, once on each eyelid. My heart is so full of love it aches, but even now it beats with a steady pulse of dread.

"Weed. I am afraid. I do not know what Oleander will do next."

He takes me in his arms and draws me close. "I

never should have left you. How could I have let you out of my sight?"

"We should flee – "

"Not yet." His fingertips trace their way down my throat, across my collarbone. "I have waited so long," he murmurs.

I freeze. The aphrodisiac is still having its effect. More slowly, now that it is faded with time, but just as surely as before.

Oleander's cruel voice snakes through my brain.

Had you forgotten, lovely? No one, not even your precious, simpering Weed, comes near you except at my pleasure.

"Weed – no – " I reach for the vial of mithridatum in hopes that it might cure him of this intoxicant – but it is empty. He has given me every drop.

Without the aid of my powerful potions, do you think this righteous bore would be mooning over you as he is now? Cooing his words of love and groaning with desire? No, lovely. He would despise you, for all you have become, and all you have done.

"My beloved," Weed whispers, unfastening my flimsy gown. "Such beauty."

How he would scorn you! This carnival huckster who makes virgin buds open on command – what use would he have for a blossom so thoroughly spent and trampled upon as you? Show me a bee in England who has not already tasted your sweet poison nectar –

"Love me, Jessamine." Weed takes my face in his hands. "Love me as you once did. I have missed you so."

He presses his lips against mine. Our bodies cling to each other like a joining of twin souls. I am clear-headed, for the first time in months. Weed's cure has cleansed the laudanum from my system, and all of Oleander's other poisons as well.

But even as I have regained myself, Weed has succumbed. His eyes are too ablaze with passion. His breath comes too quickly. It is my own body that is poison now – it is my very nearness to him that puts him in thrall to the Prince's power.

I try to pull away. "Weed. I must leave."

"No," he murmurs into my neck. "You were lost to me, and now I have you back. I will never let you go again. I love you."

His words rain down on my soul, drop by healing drop. If only they were real! But surely the potion began its work the moment he took me in his arms. With each moment he tended to me, wiped my brow, caressed my hand as I slept, the Prince's power over him grew.

From the moment Weed first touched me, his thoughts and feelings were not his own. And when the potion wears off, I will be left to face the truth.

Will there be love in Weed's heart then? Or scorn? Hatred, even?

How could I ever dare to find out?

"I am sorry," I say hoarsely. "Let me go. Please."

"Why?" His face falls. "Do you still love me?"

Go on, lovely. Put an end to this embarrassing display. At least your last lover was a king.

"No." I push him away. "I must go. I must return to my master."

267

Now he does release me. "You mean Oleander? But service to him is worse than death."

"You should have let me die, then."

Weed's eyes are full of grief. "Jessamine, what has happened to you?"

"Everything." I clench my hands into fists to stop myself from reaching for him. "Let me alone, Weed. I am soiled with wickedness, with murder – I am not even human. I am something beyond hope."

"You have killed, but you have healed as well, I know you have. Like the plants of the apothecary garden, you are healer and killer both. As am I."

"I would have to give my life a hundred times over to make up for the lives I have taken. I wish I had died at Hulne Abbey! Then I never would have sunk into this pit. I would have died a human being, instead of a devil."

His voice catches. "But I am no better than you, Jessamine. I too have killed."

His pain moves me to tears. "Do you mean the preacher at the crossroads?" I whisper. I see I am right, for he drops his head in shame.

"The world will not forgive us," he says, "but surely we could find a way to forgive each other?"

"I forgive you, Weed." It takes all my will to back away from him. "But I can never forgive myself."

By the time he looks up I have reached the door. "No! Jessamine, stay! When there is life, there is hope."

"Not always." And then I run.

With each step I take, my soul dies within me. The pain is unbearable.

I know only one way to stop it.

18

Are you very weary, *lovely? You must be.*
Even with the help of so much laudanum, forgetting is
exhausting work. And you do have a great deal to forget.

I am weary, yes. I am too tired to think.

It has been a long journey. You have done wrong; you
have disobeyed me, and disappointed me greatly.

I am sorry.

And I was so looking forward to the moment when the
King lay dying on the floor! His loyal nobles would have
tried to kill you on the spot, and poor Weed would have
had quite a puzzle to solve – save the dying King, or defend
his beloved murderess? But you ruined my little plan.

I did not know – I did not think –

Still, you are with me now. You chose wisely, in leaving that foolish boy behind at last. I think you have suffered enough. Let me bear you on my wings now. Winter is coming. It is time to rest. I will take you someplace safe.

I no longer know what to do.

Come. Let us fly.

Here we are.

Wait – do I know this place?

As well as I know you, lovely.

Is that burned ruin Hulne Abbey? And are those the gates of the poison garden my father planted, so long ago? Wait – my father, I think I remember. He is dead, is he not? Or was that only a dream?

Let us not speak of unhappy things. You are so dear to me, Jessamine. I have watched you since you were a girl, you know. I tempted you for years, calling to you, beckoning you to come closer. Even as a child, your nearness fed my powers. Do you remember how you peered longingly through the iron bars? How badly you wanted to unlock these gates, and enter my sanctuary, and pry all *the secrets from my innermost heart? And now you are here. And you are mine. You have no one else, but you need no one else. I am mother and father to you now. I am lover and ruler. I am your sickness, and your cure.*

She looks at me, the dawn of understanding. Ah, those eyes! Pale sapphires, bejewelled with tears. Mine, now.

Oleander, I am so cold.

I know.

I love to see her shiver. It makes her glitter, like a stand of birch when the breeze blows through it.

Lie down, lovely. I want to see you among the leaves.

But the earth is nearly frozen.

Lie down, and be still.

She lies on the earth and gazes at the sky.

What now?

Wait and see.

At my command, tiny roots rise up and twine themselves around her.

No.

I want to see you dressed in lace. Like a bride.

Slowly, caressingly, the delicate roots weave

themselves around her. She lets out a little gasp. Worms rise from the earth, and slither in ecstasy across that pale flesh.

Are you afraid?

Rapid puffs of frost pant from her lips.

Silly question, I know.

I wave a hand, and the roots tickle their way over her face, until they make a living veil. A wedding mantua. She moans and closes her eyes. Little does she know: This is only the beginning of our life together.

Look at me, Jessamine. Look at me.

Disobedient girl. I crook my finger, and the roots twine around her lashes and pull her eyes wide. The panicked orbs dart around, wild with fear. Unable to even blink without my permission.

Now do you understand?

It is a moment to be cherished, when the struggling ends. When all hope is gone, and terror melts into surrender. There is a tenderness to it, as prey bares its throat to predator in supplication, pleading for a final act of love – *let my end be swift* –

I feel the joy of that moment now, as those wild,

273

brimming eyes turn to me. To whom else can they turn? I am her world now, and she is mine. But still, a gentleman must ask. On bended knee, as befits a prince taking a bride.

Will you be mine, lovely? Will you do my bidding with your whole poisoned heart?

Yes, she whispers. *Unless you will let me die.*

You know I would never do that.

With a wave I bid the roots close her eyes, and seal them. A thousand threadlike fingers run themselves through the mane of her hair. They tug, and her head tips back; she lets out a little cry. I nod, and they tighten bit by bit, from head to toe, until my prize is held fast. A mermaid caught in a fisherman's net. Mine, at last.

I gesture down, toward the earth. The roots obey me, as they must. Down into the dirt she sinks, limb by limb, until her form is hidden beneath the dark veil of earth. Only her nose and mouth remain above ground. That lovely, petal-soft mouth. Even gasping for air, rounded as a carp's, still, so very lovely.

I place a tender kiss upon those trembling lips.

Will you be mine?

Yes.

Swear it, lovely. On the life you hold most precious. I know it is not your own.

I swear. On Weed's life, I swear.

On his life, indeed. Remember that vow, if you should ever think of disobeying me again. How helpless and irresistible you are! Wrapped up so prettily in the earth, like a gift that only I can open. I am quite breathless at the sight of you, Jessamine.

Inflamed, I kiss her again, and lay myself upon her. I shelter her beneath my canopy of green. I let my form change, my leaves and stems unfurl. I am full of sap and ripening buds, roots searching for moisture, my leaves turning toward the light, but now is not the time. For winter is coming, and down, down we must go, deep into the rotting, wormy earth. Down we plunge, and my beloved is coming with me –

Dear God – Oleander – where are you taking me?

Time to go home, lovely. My home. Our home.

19

4th February

THE PORTS OF PADUA and Venice were closed after word of the attack on the King spread. There was no way out by ship, so in spite of Signora Baglioni's protests against what she called my "idiotic plan," on foot I began my journey over the mountains, through war-torn France to the port of Calais.

I saw things too terrible to describe. Heads of men on pikes at every crossroad. Mobs that roamed the streets, ready to kill anyone – man, woman, or child

– whom they thought was opposed to their cause.

I saw all but felt little. The most terrible acts of humans can scarcely compare to the evils of nature unbound.

It was not until after Jessamine ran from me and the stupor of desire faded that I realised: I too had been poisoned by some subtle means. By then she was gone.

I understood both to be Oleander's doing – the love potion, and her terrified flight. The plants of the *Orto botanico* would not tell me where he was taking her, but in my heart I knew there was only one answer: He would take her to England. To Northumberland. To the poison garden.

That is where I am bound.

The hellish garden has possessed my dreams. Each day I fight sleep as long as I can, for the moment I close my eyes the nightmare returns: the poison garden, made bleak by winter. Bare branches, dead stalks. The ground is thick with snow, except for one spot, where ice will not form.

In the dream I have wings, like Oleander's. I descend, and lay my hand upon the spot. Everywhere else the earth is frozen. Here it is warm as flesh.

Across the whole of the north of England the snow comes down. It blankets the fields and forms tall drifts. Yet in this spot alone, the flakes melt the instant they touch the earth, revealing again and again the terrible outline: the shape of a girl's body, splayed on the barren ground.

He has taken her! I shout it to the forest and fields. But the evergreens slumber, and the leafy plants, too, are resting below.

I lay myself up on the spot, and fit my limbs to the place where my beloved once lay. Senseless to the cold, I let the snow cover me. I cling to the ground as if the world would try to throw me off and send me flying out into the heavens.

I press my lips to the earth and call her name, again and again, until my mouth fills with dirt and my tears turn to ice on my cheeks.

Jessamine – Jessamine – Jessamine!

That is when I awaken, always. Shivering with a cold that knows no end. The bitter cold of a winter that may never more see spring.

I draw my cloak around me, and go on. Soon I will reach Calais. If the winds and weather permit, a half-day's sail will take me across the Channel to Dover. Then by land I will make my way to Northumberland. What awaits me there, God and the devil only know.

From the low grey sky, hour by hour, the snow continues to fall.